DECK THE SHELVES

TONI SHILOH

Cover design by Toni Shiloh.

Published in the United States of America by Toni Shiloh.

www.ToniShiloh.wordpress.com

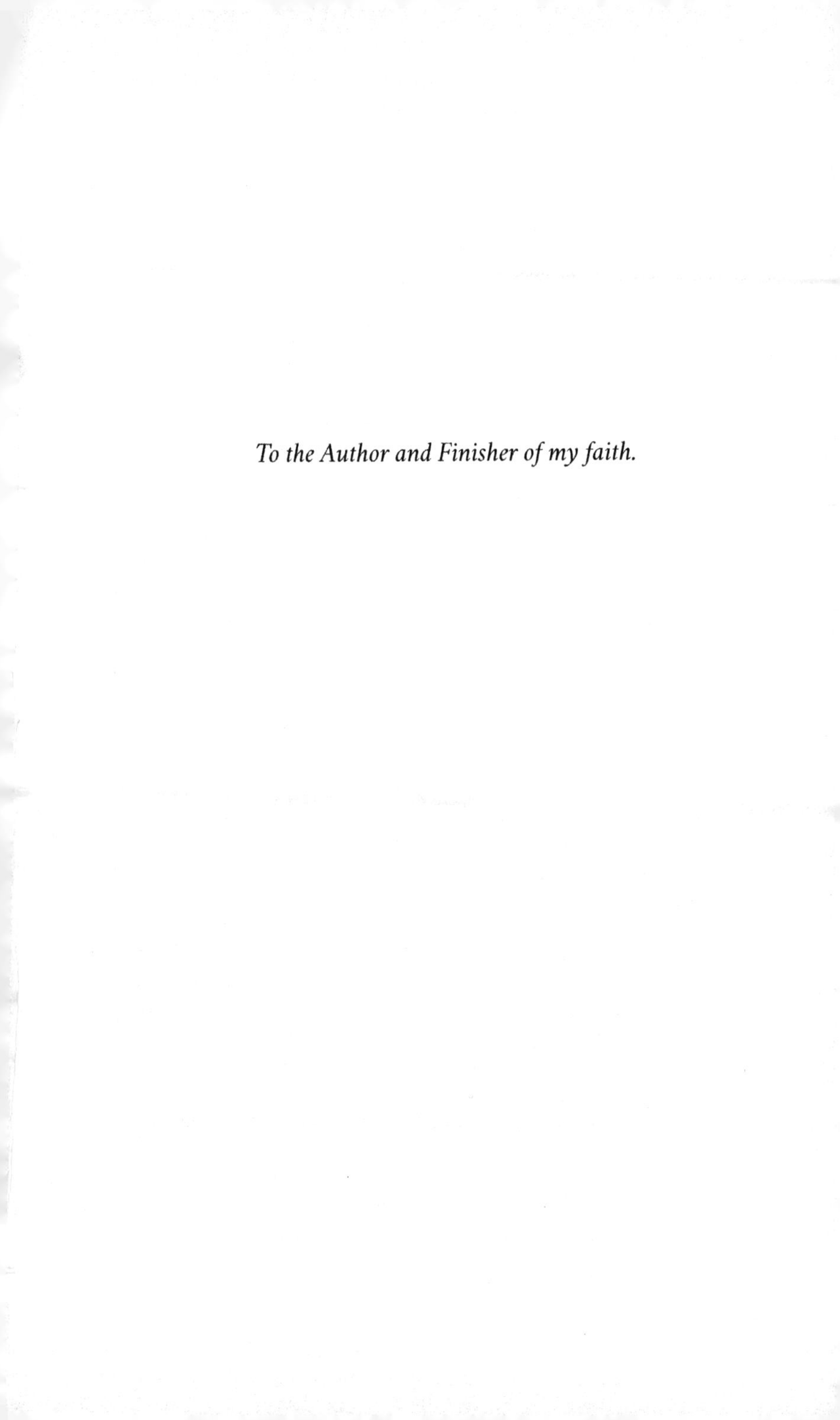

To the Author and Finisher of my faith.

Chapter One

"But a Book is only the Heart's Portrait- every Page a Pulse." —
Emily Dickinson

Quinton Hendricks entered the red-brick Victorian aptly named The Cozy Shelf. He peeked into the arched doorway on his right, checking for Kendall at the checkout counter. His heart dipped into disappointment at her absence. *Probably helping a customer.* Question was should he find her or look busy until she came back?

He entered the room and walked to the gift area. Kendall always had interesting paraphernalia for all things book related. Besides, it afforded him the perfect view to watch for her return. It was better than roaming around the bookstore trying to locate her. A mug that read "Just One More Chapter" caught his attention. With a grin, he grabbed it. Gran would love it, and if he could purchase a book by her favorite author as well, then she'd be crossed off his Christmas list.

Light whistling greeted his ears as footfalls drew closer. He straightened to his full height and twisted, staring at the doorway that led to the rest of the bookstore. He inhaled sharply as the object of his affection crossed the threshold.

Kendall Jackson's pale pink lips curved upward and laugh lines appeared, framing her perfect mouth. "Morning, Q. Are you ready to check out and purchase anything?" Her light-brown skin glowed under the recessed lighting in the ceiling.

"Actually, no." He walked over to the wooden counter. "I just started in here. Haven't moved to the other rooms yet." His lips quirked up to the right. "Your shirt matches my mug." He showed her the one he'd picked out.

"I love that mug." She glanced to her right, taking in the gift area. "I love them all really."

"I'm looking for a book for Gran. Have any recommendations?"

"Of course." She straightened, tugging at her book-shaped earrings. "Her favorite author just had a new book release. Follow me."

To the ends of the earth. He shook his head, erasing the cobwebs that fogged his brain whenever she drew near. Kendall never saw him as anything other than a frequent customer. He'd done everything he could think of to gain her attention short of asking her out.

And why haven't you? You like her, ask her out.

But it wasn't that simple. He had Deuce to look after.

Dating as a single parent wasn't just about himself. He had to make sure that whatever he did left a good impression on his son. Or rather, it was the reasoning he gave himself for not asking Kendall out.

Lame, Q.

She crossed the front entrance and entered the room across the hall with the *Fresh Fiction* placard above the doorway. A reader could find any book written in a present-day setting. Kendall stopped in front of a bookshelf which almost reached the ceiling but left enough space for a placard that read *Romance*. A footstool sat in the aisle not too far away.

"She loves Beverly Jenkins." Kendall scanned the air with her pointer finger as she searched.

He reached over her and pointed. "Right there. Which one is the new one?" He'd never even heard of Beverly Jenkins. Then again, when he had an opportunity to read it was auto mechanic magazines or children's books.

"*Second Time Sweeter* is the latest book in her Blessings series." Kendall reached for it.

"I got it." He tried not to invade her space as he grabbed the book off of the shelf. But man was it difficult not to. Her scent reminded him of a warm winter's night. *Intoxicating.*

Her curls had been gathered into a ponytail on top of her head. The smell of her shampoo seemed to mix into the signature fragrance that was pure Kendall.

"Q?"

"Sorry." He gulped, backing up with the book in hand. "I'll take this and the mug." And hurry outside where the fall weather could cool him off.

So far this year, the town of Heartfalls had been spared early winter weather. Of course, in November central New York usually started receiving snowstorms. Right now, he was just thankful for temperatures in the fifties. He'd need the slap of the wind after leaving The Cozy Shelf.

"Do you need a gift bag?" Kendall asked as she scanned the items with her cell.

Quinton glanced at the gift bags. "I don't suppose you have some bookish wrapping paper or something to that effect?"

"Come on, Q. You know better than that." Kendall winked at him. "They're over there."

She walked past the gift bags and pointed at the various wrapping papers along the wall display. One was red and green with the word *Book* all over. Instead, he opted for the black-and-white wrapping paper that had classic titles all over it.

"Fantastic," Kendall beamed at him. She swiveled her iPad on the stand to allow him to swipe his credit card and complete his purchase.

He couldn't believe you could pay for items using an iPad nowadays. "Thanks, Kendall."

"Sure thing. See you tomorrow?" She tilted her head in question.

"Most likely." *Definitely.*

With a wave good-bye, he left the room, and then the store. A groan tore from his lips. "Another missed chance, Q boy."

He shook his head and opened the door of his work in progress. His 1949 Ford F1 truck still needed restoration done in parts of the vehicle, but it was drivable. Once he and his father finished, it would be a beaut. Instead, the red-rusted exterior left much to be desired.

Quinton cruised down the streets of Heartfalls, taking in the familiar sights and the leaves which covered the streets. He'd been born and raised in the college town. Except for a four-year stint in the Air Force, he'd remained. His family still lived here. His work—Hendricks and Sons Auto—gave him purpose. Life was good, and he couldn't, no *shouldn't,* complain. Except...

He wanted a relationship with Kendall. Or at least the possibility to see where it could go. The wounds of his divorce had healed, and he wanted to date again. At least he thought he did. The fear of rejection was strong since his ex-wife had packed a bag and left him and Deuce to fend for themselves. When they'd first met, he would have never imagined her capable of abandonment. What if he was wrong about Kendall?

Yet something about her wiggled its way into his heart. Had it beating faster in her presence. And he'd be lying if he hadn't thought of his son and the need for a woman in Deuce's life. Stacy sure didn't want any part in raising Quinton, Jr., and his gran was getting up there in age. She could love on Deuce and read stories, but she couldn't be a mom.

Lord, please give me an idea, some way to get Kendall's attention and let her know how I feel.

Kendall stared blankly at the door. The first time Quinton Hendricks had walked into her bookstore, her heart had done some strange flip. She'd blamed it on the dragon noodles that'd been the day's lunch. But when her heart continued to flip at every sighting of Q, she could no longer deny the attraction.

Crazy how she'd thought he felt the same way. He'd went from coming in every week to every other day, and now he was in her shop daily. Not once had he asked her out. Obviously, she'd made a mountain out of a molehill. She was reminded of the quote from *Pride and Prejudice.*

"A lady's imagination is very rapid; it jumps from admiration to love, from love to matrimony in a moment."

Not that she was thinking marriage. She'd settle for a date with the handsome mechanic. His warm brown eyes always seemed to shine with joy. And the way the laugh lines fanned out made her want to smile. His strong jaw had a cleft chin—her one weakness—covered by a night's worth of stubble. The single father made her dream upon dreams.

She sighed, placing her chin in her hand. One of her best friends had urged Kendall to take matters into her own hands. Daisy thought asking a guy out would take away the pressure, but Kendall didn't want to be the one asking. Call her old-fashioned, but she wanted a romance worthy of the classics. For their eyes to meet and hearts understand what the mind couldn't. Of course, she'd rather skip all the drama and subterfuge that went with the classics. But still, a great love that stood the test of time and had readers across the world uniting for #teamgilbert, #teamdarcy, and countless other heroes worthy of admiration.

The brass shop bell jingled as the door opened ushering in Daisy Tate and her daughter. It was like her mind conjured up her friend. Daisy held Bliss's hand, who had on a pair of miniature UGG boots. Bliss had to be the cutest four-year-old Kendall had ever seen. Her light brown curls framed an angelic face with chubby cheeks.

"Hey, girl." Kendall rounded the counter and enveloped her friend in a hug. "How are you?"

"Tired."

"Grab a cup of coffee."

"Good idea. Can you watch Bliss?"

"Sure thing." Kendall scooped the little girl up in her arms, tickling her.

Daisy wandered out to the foyer where the hospitality table was set up. Every morning, Kendall grabbed a selection of K-cups and readied the hot water for the tea drinkers. This morning, she'd made blueberry scones and gluten-free muffins.

Kendall leaned against the wall, watching her friend. "How's everything?"

"Rough. Bliss woke up at three this morning." She eyed her daughter. "Climbed into our bed and activated the ring of her toy phone."

Kendall's shoulders shook with suppressed laughter. "Who jumped awake first?"

"Girl, please. Sean sleeps like the dead. It's a good thing I'd already used the bathroom an hour earlier or there would have been a mess to clean up."

Kendall couldn't hold back her laughter any longer. Bliss looked at her and giggled along. "No, ma'am." She shook her head at the little girl. "You're the reason for the bags under your poor mama's eyes." She glanced at Daisy. "Did you scare Bliss, jumping like a mad woman?"

"Please, that girl was giggling like a hyena this morning."

"And Sean really slept through it?"

"Yep. Had the nerve to wake up all refreshed and ready to go this morning." Daisy grabbed her mug from the open-faced cup display. "Like it's not a Monday and we don't have a preschooler who doesn't understand playtime is for daylight hours only."

Daisy and Sean had tied the knot eight years ago, right after college graduation. It had taken them awhile to get pregnant. Kendall knew Daisy wanted more children, but so far, Bliss was it.

"Did she go back to sleep?"

"After an hour. Then woke back up at six."

"Yuck." As much as Kendall wanted a family of her own, waking up that early did not sound good. She was all about sleep, when she wasn't reading of course.

"How's your day going? Shop seems quiet."

"Ms. Redderman is curled up with a book somewhere. A few people have been in for coffee."

"You should start charging."

"Nah." That wasn't her style.

Daisy rolled her eyes and shook her head, downing the rest of her coffee. "Well, I'm going to buy Bliss a book, so I don't feel so guilty."

"You're not obligated to buy something every time you walk in here, Daisy."

"I do it for support."

Kendall put an arm around Daisy's shoulders. "And I appreciate that."

"Did your *friend* come in yet?" Daisy's dark eyes sparkled with mirth.

She nodded and pivoted, hoping Daisy didn't catch the

blush warming her face. "He bought something for his grandmother."

"How much money does the man have?"

"He doesn't buy something every day." Kendall tilted her head. Come to think of it, he *had* bought something every day last week. "Or maybe he does."

Daisy nudged her. "That's because he likes you, Kendall."

"He's never hinted at it."

"What do you think plunking down money every single day is?"

Her face warmed. "Maybe he's a bookworm."

"Has he purchased something for himself?"

"An auto magazine."

"So not bookish at all."

She shrugged. Q came in every day. He had to have some love of books in him somewhere, *right*?

"I can see those wheels turning. I'm telling you he likes you."

"But..."

"But what?" Daisy took Bliss, settling her onto her hip.

"Why hasn't he asked me out?"

"Maybe he's shy like you are?"

That would *not* do. How were two shy people supposed to get together? Not that she was shy. More like traditional.

"How can I encourage him?"

"Ask him out."

Her nose wrinkled.

"Then at least tell the man you like him." Daisy huffed.

"Can't do that either." Her stomach knotted.

"Then I guess you better send up a prayer because I'm at a lost."

Kendall nodded as her mind focused on God. *Lord, you know how much I've thought about Q. You know how much my mind has jumped to dreams and had us living happily ever after. Lord, please move in this situation and reign my thoughts under Your will. In Jesus' name, Amen.*

Chapter Two

"There is nothing in the world so irresistibly contagious as laughter and good humor."— Charles Dickens, *A Christmas Carol*

The sound of delighted giggles reached Quinton's ears as he opened the front door. He stopped in the doorway to the living room, taking in the picture of Deuce smiling and clapping his hands with amusement.

"Again, Gran, again!"

His grandmother repeated the words of the big, bad wolf, puffing her cheeks out to blow air against Deuce's face. His son fell back, giggling as if it was the most hilarious thing in the world. Sadness tapped against the joy in the room. He hated that Deuce didn't have a mother, but he loved that his grandmother had stepped into the role as much as her rheumatoid arthritis would allow her.

Her gnarled hands turned the page until she came to

the end. When she snapped the book closed, Deuce looked up and froze. His big eyes widened, and he jumped off her lap.

"Daddy!"

"Hey, Deuce!" He threw his son up in the air to hear his laughter one more time before hugging him close. "Did you eat your breakfast?"

"Uh-huh."

"Did you drink your juice?"

Deuce nodded his head vigorously.

"Good boy."

Quinton set his son down and walked over to his grandmother. He laid a kiss on her cheek. "Morning, Gran."

"Morning, Q. How's our bookstore owner?"

He rubbed the heat out of the back of his neck. "Kendall's good."

"I bet she looked pretty this morning."

Doesn't she always? He nodded, avoiding the knowing look that was sure to be in Gran's eyes.

"Have you asked her out?"

"No," he groaned as he sank into the leather recliner.

"Why not?"

"I don't know, Gran. I get so tongue tied around her. What if she doesn't like me that way?"

"Q baby, you'll never know unless you ask her."

"I wish there was a way to gauge her interest before..." He shrugged his shoulders, not sure he really knew what he meant.

"Well..." Gran drew out.

Q glanced at his grandmother. "Do you have an idea?"

"Why don't you leave her a note. Like from a secret

admirer. You could leave them in various places around The Cozy Shelf. Places Kendall will be sure to spot them."

He rubbed his stubble, subconsciously noting the need for a shave. "That could work. But what would I write in the notes, Gran? I'm not a poet."

"No, but maybe you could let the classic poets and writers speak for you. Kind of a Cyrano de Bergerac thing going on."

"Who?"

Gran chuckled, mirth filling her aged eyes. The brown color was now ringed with gray. He hated to see his grandmother age, but she refused to let the body "trap" her, as she was always saying.

"He liked a special woman and felt inadequate to tell her because of an unsightly facial feature. Needless to say, he persevered in the end."

"So just look up old poets for inspiration?"

"Yes, I'm sure she would love it. Maybe you could even find out her favorites."

"How?"

"Pay attention to the girl, and I'm sure you'll figure it out."

"Thanks, Gran." He rose. "Will you be okay with Deuce today?" Some days a neighbor had to watch Deuce when his grandmother's RA flared.

"I'm good today," she beamed, wrinkles lining her mouth.

"Thanks, Gran." He kissed her on the forehead and straightened. "Deuce," he shouted.

"Comin', Daddy."

His son barreled into his legs. "I'm off to work, kiddo."

"'Kay. I'll be good."

Q bent down. "I know you will. Can I get a hug goodbye?"

"Always, Daddy."

He pulled his namesake in, relishing in the trust Deuce had for him. Other parents said the time flew by, so he would soak in these moments when his son still wanted to be around him. "See you later, buddy."

"Bye, Daddy."

Quinton high fived his son and went out the front door once more. This time to head in to Hendricks and Sons Auto Shop.

In high school, Q had been so excited when he became a working member of society. And the day his father took down the old Hendricks Auto Shop sign to add *and Sons*, he'd been moved to tears. His father had been the same, but it wasn't his way to display emotion. Instead, he'd clapped Q on the back and had begun working on the next car.

Backing out of the driveway, Quinton paused to glance over at the black sided home with white shutters. The one his grandmother had raised his father in and now helped usher in another generation with Deuce. He needed to rake the leaves the trees had rained down around the yard.

Shaking himself from his musing, Q put the car in drive and slowly cruised down Falls Creek Avenue. The neighborhood had a lot of older families. Toward the end of the block, younger families were moving in. The college crowd of ten years ago were becoming parents. A lot of the students from Heartfalls University stayed in the area, choosing to take some of the jobs available close by.

It was a good time to be a small business owner and a good place to own a business. The shop never lacked for work, keeping his family in much needed funds. He wondered how The Cozy Shelf faired. Maybe it was something he could talk to Kendall about, open a doorway for more substantial conversation.

He tapped the steering wheel as he turned down the road leading to the shop. Gran's suggestion of notes placed in the bookstore held a lot of appeal. He could gauge Kendall's reaction to them, maybe even see if it came up in everyday conversation. Then he could do a big reveal if the response pointed in his favor. Maybe near Christmas considering it was a month away.

Lord, can I do this? Become a secret admirer? Is that wrong? How can I use it to get to know Kendall better?

And more importantly, was he truly ready for another relationship?

~

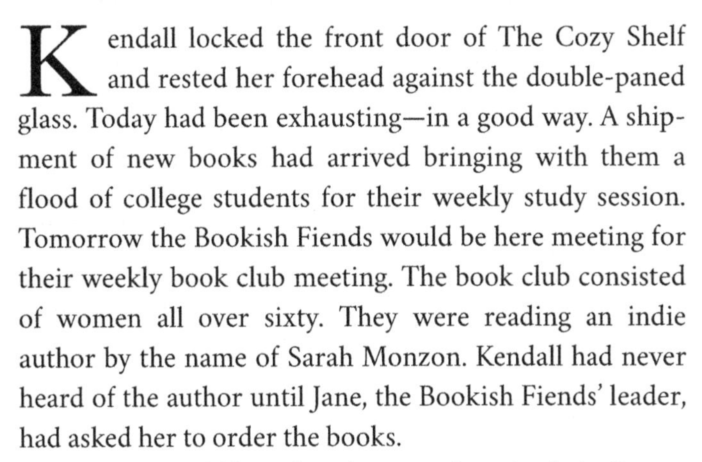

Kendall locked the front door of The Cozy Shelf and rested her forehead against the double-paned glass. Today had been exhausting—in a good way. A shipment of new books had arrived bringing with them a flood of college students for their weekly study session. Tomorrow the Bookish Fiends would be here meeting for their weekly book club meeting. The book club consisted of women all over sixty. They were reading an indie author by the name of Sarah Monzon. Kendall had never heard of the author until Jane, the Bookish Fiends' leader, had asked her to order the books.

Kendall would have loved to join them in their discussion, but running the store took all her time. Instead she'd read *The Esther Paradigm,* a modern twist on the book of Esther, at night. The romantic tale had gripped her from the opening pages as it took her to the Middle East. To top it off, it was a Christian romance. Kendall loved how the author wove wisdom and faith in between the pages. She'd promptly ordered the rest of the authors' works to add to her personal collection.

Kendall flicked on the security lights and headed for the foyer. The circular staircase sat in the back of the alcove. She climbed the steps, stopping on the second-floor landing where the Adventure Cove room, book club meeting area, and literature sections beckoned. She glanced into each room to make sure they were clean. A book had been left in the window seat of Masterpiece Corner. Tiffany helped her in the afternoons and was usually pretty good at straightening up before leaving.

Then again, the young woman had stars in her eyes when her boyfriend showed up ten minutes before her shift had ended. Kendall climbed the stairs to the third and final floor, the residential floor or, as she liked to call it, the flat. When she'd inherited the place from her grandmother, Kendall had made the decision to turn the third floor into her apartment versus living elsewhere. Her mother had thought it was a mistake. Something about not living near your work.

But Kendall loved everything about the one-hundred-and-twenty-five-year old Victorian home. She unlocked the door to her flat and walked in, setting the keys on the *Go Away I'm Reading* key hook.

"Meow."

"Good evening, Lady Catherine."

The white Persian blinked and pivoted, giving her the cold shoulder.

Kendall chuckled. "I get it. Let's get your dinner."

The kitchen—if one could even call it that as it sat along one wall—had all the appliances she needed. A microwave, stove, and oven. Of course, there was no designated pantry or even a decent amount of cupboard space. She pulled a can of cat food out of the cupboards and popped the top.

"Meow." Lady Catherine weaved in between her feet, showing her pleasure.

Kendall placed the food in a dish and set it on the floor. "Enjoy." She peered into the pantry. "Now what am I going to eat?" After being on her feet all day, she really wanted to sit down. So, she grabbed a bowl and a box of Lucky Charms.

After pouring the milk, Kendall headed to her over-stuffed chair. It had probably been the end piece of a sectional, but she'd found it alone at a thrift shop. She curled under her favorite literary fleece blanket. It had the words of *Pride and Prejudice* written all over it and was soft and warm.

Lady Catherine pranced out of the kitchen and sat in her tower. She blinked at Kendall, communicating her need for background noise and a good nap. Happy to oblige, Kendall opened her laptop and clicked on the Netflix icon. She needed something good to watch, but not so good that it would distract her from finishing the latest Ronie Kendig book.

She picked a Netflix original and grabbed her book, pulling the bookmark out at the same time. She read the first sentence and her cell rang.

"No," she moaned.

The old-fashioned ring continued as she fumbled to swipe her cell open while balancing her cereal and book. "Hello?" she breathed out.

"Kendall, how are you?"

"Mom?" She sat up. "Where are you?"

"I'm in Dublin. Our plane had some mechanical issues, so we've been put up in a hotel for the night."

"Are you okay?"

"Nothing serious. The door was malfunctioning."

Considering one needed it to maintain cabin pressure, it seemed pretty serious to her. Still, her mom seemed calm about it. "Did you do any sightseeing?"

"No. I should be asleep, but I'm still on East coast time. I figured you'd be awake and thought I'd call to say hi."

Kendall had a weird relationship with her mother. It wasn't a bad relationship, but it wasn't the warmest one either. Her mother had been a flight attendant for as long as she could remember. When Kendall's father refused to accept Kendall as his own, her mother had gotten the first job she could, desperate for funds. She'd flown until the airline had put her on maternity leave. Six weeks after giving birth she'd gone right back, leaving Kendall with her grandmother.

Her mother was like some magical figure that popped into her life at random, bringing trinkets and gifts from around the world. Sometimes she'd stay for a day but most often she was gone in time to catch another flight.

"I appreciate you calling."

"Are you reading?"

"I am. You?"

"I'm probably going to watch a Netflix movie or binge

some show until I fall asleep."

"Oh." Silence filled the air as Kendall scrambled for something to say. "How's the weather?"

"It's a little damp but nothing terrible."

"It's been clear here. No sign of rain or snow." She took a bite of her cereal, trying to minimize the crunch.

"What's that noise?"

"Sorry," she spoke around the cereal, and then swallowed the bite down. "I just took a bite of cereal."

"Really?" Her mom laughed. "I thought eating cereal late at night was my thing."

Her mom ate cereal for dinner? Kendall smiled. So, she did have something in common with her after all.

"I don't know why but I love Lucky Charms. I always carry the individual packs with me when I go on a trip."

"That's what I'm eating, too."

"Like mother like daughter." Her mom paused. "Listen, I have some vacation time coming next month. I'm sorry I can't be there for Thanksgiving, but maybe you and I could get together for Christmas?"

"I'd like that," she said softly. When was the last time they'd had Christmas together?

"Great. When it gets closer, I'll call with more details. I'll get a room at the hotel or maybe do an Airbnb."

Kendall looked around her flat. There really was no place to put her mom unless they were going to share her queen-sized bed. "Makes sense."

"Love you, Kendall."

"Love you, too." She hung up, staring mindlessly at the screen.

For the first time in years, she wouldn't be alone for Christmas.

Chapter Three

"I know nothing in the world that has as much power as a word. Sometimes I write one, and I look at it, until it begins to shine."

— Emily Dickinson

Q walked down the ramp and underneath the undercarriage of the Audi A3 on the lift. Brian had brought his vehicle in for a routine oil change. The man sat in the air-conditioned waiting room with a cup of joe from their old-fashioned coffee maker. Q's father refused to get a Keurig and come into the 21st century.

Footfalls reached his ears as he loosened the drain bolt.

"Q? Is that you?"

He turned around and smiled from underneath the Audi. "Professor, my man, how's it going?" Quinton greeted, using Xavier's nickname as Q walked up the ramp.

"Not bad. You?" Xavier asked, hooking his thumbs in his belt loops.

"Pretty good."

Xavier motioned to the Audi with his head. "That's a sweet ride."

"I'm partial to my truck."

He chuckled. "You get any more work done on the refurbishment?"

"The outside is all good. Waiting on interior pieces to come."

"Nice."

Q folded his arms. "It's nice for you to drop by, but I have a feeling you're here for a reason."

"I've been thinking, and I believe God is calling me to step into a volunteer role at church."

"Yes." Q grinned. He'd been waiting for the moment Professor would step into his calling. His boy had a way with the Word, always bringing enlightenment to the men's group at church. Q and other church leaders had asked him to lead a time or two, but Xavier always said no, claiming to be unqualified.

"Are you thinking of leading a study?" Q asked.

"Actually, I'm leaning towards helping with the youth."

"The youth?" His eyebrows raised. "Huh," he rubbed the stubble along his chin, thinking.

"It's a bad idea, isn't it?" Xavier's shoulders slumped, stooping his six-foot frame.

"Nah, I actually really like the idea. You have a lot of experience that could be used to reinforce the power of sticking to the right path."

"Don't you mean the opposite?"

"Professor, your experience makes you an expert. No, you didn't stick to the right path, but you can share how you wish you had. But don't forget to remind them of the glorious testament of God's grace in case they already feel like they're on the wrong path. You want them to choose God, but you also want to offer a road of redemption if they've already rejected Him."

Xavier nodded, rocking back on the heels of his feet. "I'm tracking with you."

"We're doing a lock-in next week." Q continued. "I know it's short notice, but we have to do it then, otherwise we run into Thanksgiving and everyone's winter plans. Anyway, why don't you come as a chaperone? We'll be breaking into small groups during the lock-in so you'll have an opportunity to build relationships."

"I want to say no, Q, but God's telling me to say yes."

"Then you know what to do."

Professor nodded. "Thanks, man."

"Anytime."

"Enough about me." Xavier folded his arms across his chest. "What's going on with you?"

"Not much."

"You still visiting The Cozy Shelf every day?"

Q's face warmed under the Professor's scrutiny. He had visited again this morning, grabbing a book for his son called *When Daddy Prays*. It would be a great book to read before Deuce's bedtime. Of course, he wouldn't share it with him until Christmas morning. "I dropped by this morning."

"When are you going to get over that hump and ask her out?"

He sighed. "Gran actually gave me an idea." Q told him of his plan. "What do you think?"

"I think it sounds perfect."

"I'm not book smart like you two. How am I going to figure out which book to quote from?"

"Internet. A quick search will pull up links to hundreds of quotes. Spend a little time looking for one that speaks to the words in your heart. Words are powerful things, man."

"Yeah, I can do that." Q spun the wrench in his hand. "Xavier, do you think we're too different? Kendall's smart. Runs her own business and reads. *A lot.*"

"Not at all. You run your own business too."

"Yeah, with my dad." Nothing about his life said he could make his own way without help.

"As a *partner.* Wouldn't you love it if Deuce worked with you one day?"

He nodded. *So maybe I'm making a big deal out of nothing.*

Xavier continued. "You're a father and that takes a special wisdom to raise a man in this world who will believe in God. Trust me, I know from lack of experience. I had no father to show me the right path." His jaw tightened.

"Thanks." Q only spoke to give Xavier some time to compose himself.

"Find out her favorite book and go from there. I'm sure you can find a way to leave her the notes and still hint to who they're from."

"Appreciate that, man. And I'll let you know when the next youth lock-in meeting is."

"See you round, Q."

"Later, Professor."

Quinton lowered the Audi to finish his work. As his hands mindlessly took the necessary steps to complete his task, his mind wondered. His ex-wife's abandonment had left him feeling inadequate. How could he be enough for any woman when the one who'd vowed to be with him until death had bounced at the first opportunity? It had taken him awhile to even begin looking at other women. The day Kendall opened her shop had changed his life forever.

Lord, help me get over this fear of rejection. Please lead me to the perfect words to let her know how I feel. Amen.

Kendall wrapped the colorful bookshelf scarf around her hair, fluffing her curls at the top. She grabbed a red blazer to go over her black t-shirt as while slipping on her red ballet flats. She palmed her things and headed out the flat's door. The image of Quinton declaring his undying love over candlelight had filled her dreams.

The dream left her feeling a little foolish when she woke, but at the same time, a tug in her spirit told Kendall she had to do something about it.

But what, Lord?

Placing the serving bowl full of lemon poppy seed muffins on the hospitality table, Kendall sat the hot water boiler next to the Keurig. She ran up the stairs to grab the gluten-free apple muffins made from a recipe she'd discovered on Pinterest. The one she'd eaten this morning tasted fine to her, and hopefully today's patrons would agree.

Once the hospitality table was set up, Kendall flipped the *Open* sign. Soon, she'd have to break out all the Christmas decorations from storage. Usually she put the decor up the day after Thanksgiving. The shop would be closed that day, giving her the perfect opportunity to deck her shelves. But for some reason, the thought didn't hold its usual appeal.

Because you can't get Q out of your mind.

She grimaced. It was true. Even now, she ignored the urge to glance outside and see if his rusty truck would be parked alongside the curb. Did he like coffee? He hadn't claimed a space in the mug cabinet for his own cup. She never saw him with a disposable one either and she'd been too chicken to stalk him whenever he neared the hospitality table. Perhaps he was a water drinker.

The bell chimed above the door and Kendall moved to the doorway between the gift shop and foyer. Emma, Heartfalls' beloved high school principal, headed for the hospitality table. She grabbed her mug which sported an apple on top of a stack of books.

"Morning, Em."

"Ugh." She blew across the mug of coffee and took a cautious sip. After repeating the process a couple more times, she glanced toward Kendall. "Morning."

"Rough night?"

"The worst."

Kendall couldn't tell. Emma's brown skin glowed. Her makeup, flawless and understated, enhanced the beauty of her complexion. Emma's long black hair fell straight with loose curls at the end. Her cream-colored blouse was tucked neatly into a black pencil skirt.

"You do know it's Saturday, right?"

Emma froze, dark brown eyes blinking rapidly. "Are you serious?"

"No." Kendall laughed. "It's Tuesday."

"Girl," Emma drew out. "Don't scare me like that." She glanced at her rose-gold wristwatch. "I've got to be at the school in thirty minutes."

"Why so late?" She thought Emma was usually there first thing.

"I have some administration meetings. We'll talk and then do a tour of the school."

"Routine?"

"You never know with them."

"I'll pray for you."

Emma tilted her head, a soft smile gracing her lips. "Thanks, girl. How are you? Q stop by yet?"

As much as Kendall loved her friends, she really wished they'd stop asking that. "I'm good. My mother's coming for Christmas."

Her browed furrowed. "Is that a good thing?"

"I won't be alone." Kendall shrugged. "Could be worse."

"You could always stay with me. I'm not going on vacation this year."

"And likewise. You can have dinner with me and my mom."

"Thanks." She gave Kendall a side hug and pulled back. "You still didn't answer me about Q."

"No, he hasn't been by." It was still early.

"Maybe the shop is busy."

"Probably." Or maybe he was tired of coming in and getting no sign of interest from her in return. "Do you think I should ask him out?"

"That's not your style." Emma rolled her eyes. "Did Daisy suggest that?"

Why did her two favorite people hate each other? Or at least dislike one another intensely? "Yes."

"Ignore her. That's not your style."

"But what if he thinks I'm not interested. Shouldn't I give some kind of hint? Maybe flirt with him?"

"And how long did it take you to talk to him without being nervous?"

True. "Then what should I do, Emma?"

"I know." She straightened, setting her coffee mug down. "Write him a note. Whenever he comes in and buys something, slip it in his gift bag. He'll get the hint then."

An absolutely terrifying idea, yet perfect all at the same time. "And say what? I like you, do you like me, check yes or no?"

Her friend snorted with laughter. "Love it. If that's what you want to write, do it."

"I'm not sure what to write."

"You own a bookstore and can't figure it out?"

"Good point." Kendall folded her arms across her chest. "I could always take a quote or two from the classics. You know, so I'm not obvious."

"Classy." Emma winked.

"You're extra corny today."

"More like delirious. I may need to pour a refill before I leave."

"Go for it."

"Before I forget." Emma held a finger up and opened her soft pink Kate Spade tote. She pulled out a tin jar that had paper wrapped around it with wording.

"What does it say?" Kendall squinted, scooting closer. Her mouth dropped at the word: tips.

"Kendall, you have got to stop letting people take coffee and muffins for free."

"That's one thing you and Daisy seem to agree on."

"At least she's got that right." Emma popped in another K cup. "I'm going to take this and run. Don't worry, my tip is already in there."

"Thanks, girl." Kendall hugged her. "Stop by after work?"

"If I'm alive." Emma grabbed her cup and wiggled her fingers as she headed for the door.

Kendall walked up the stairs. Perhaps the Masterpiece Corner had a suggestion for her. She didn't want the note to be a simple check yes or no. It was too vulnerable and almost too forward. But a little quote from a book could be a subtle hint. One she hoped Q would pick up on.

Her hands ran across the spines of the books. Some were worn from previous ownership. Others fresh and reprinted, the classics never wavering from the public's favor. She perused the works of Jane Austen. Miss Austen always had something profound to say. She pulled *Sense and Sensibility* from the shelf. What could she learn from the two sisters?

She flipped through the pages searching for one of her favorite passages. The words jumped from the page. *"If I could but know his heart, everything would become easy."*

And wasn't that the truth? She didn't know Q's heart.

And was afraid to share her own. But if she could give him a clue and it aligned with his feelings, everything *would* be easier. Kendall closed the book. She had a lot of work to do.

Chapter Four

"Some books are so familiar that reading them is like being home again." — Louisa May Alcott

The warm soapy water relaxed the tension from Quinton's hands. He'd already used GOJO to get the grime and oil off at the shop's sink; however, washing with Dawn dish soap was his extra step once he made it to the mudroom sink in his home. Still, the stain from being an auto mechanic would linger on his fingers. He glanced at the clock above the sink. *4:00pm.* The children's story time at The Cozy Shelf would be starting in thirty minutes. That gave him time to quickly shower and change so that Deuce could hear today's story.

He hadn't been able to stop by the store in two days. An influx of work had kept him and his father busy at the auto shop. But he never missed story time, no matter how much work awaited them. It was something he and his father agreed on when his ex-wife had deserted them.

After putting on a clean Henley and exchanging his work boots for casual ones, Q headed for the living room. Deuce sat in front of the TV watching Wild Kratts, the animated animal show. Next to cars, animals were Deuce's favorite subject to talk about.

"Hey, Deuce. Ready for story time?"

"Yes," his eyes widened, and he jumped up from the floor. "Will Ms. Kendall be reading?"

I hope so. "Maybe or Tiffany."

"I like it when Ms. Kendall reads," Deuce wrapped his arms around Q's legs.

"Me too, buddy. Let's go."

"Okay, Daddy." Deuce slipped his hands in Q's. "Will you buy me a book?"

"Sure will." And he'd already tucked a note into his back pocket. He'd find someplace to leave it in Adventure Cove, the name of the children's room.

"Yay!" Deuce bounced up and down, yanking on Q's arm in exuberance.

As they drew closer to the bookstore, Quinton grimaced. All the curbside parking spots had been filled. The moms would be out in full force for story time, which meant he'd have to park in the adjacent lot or across the street in The Sweet Spot's parking lot. The dessert store was famous in Heartfalls for their cupcakes.

A quick glance told him there were still a few spots left in the adjacent lot. He wheeled his truck into the lot, aiming for the open space in the back. It would do Deuce good to run his energy out before settling down for the story.

Kendall was good for choosing a book that held a Christian worldview or represented those beliefs, despite the wide-range of books she sold. He thought she did a remarkable job at providing lots of books for every type of reader, but not to the detriment of her moral beliefs. Deuce ran down the sidewalk leading to the store's front door.

Quinton took in the pale red brick of the Victorian home. The bay window to the right was framed in black, giving a view to the gift center. The large rectangular window on the left offered a view of the modern nook, housing all the contemporary authors. Each floor had two sets of windows, letting the light shine from out. It would look amazing once Kendall decorated for the Christmas season.

He opened the front door, smiling as the bells clanged. It was so typical of her style and vibe of The Cozy Shelf. A quiet hum of activity pulsed through the atmosphere. Q headed for the stairs, so he could grab a great spot to sit while Deuce listened to story time. His son didn't want to sit in his lap like some of the other children, instead he always took a seat on the floor right in the front while Q sat in one of the chairs along the side.

What he really wanted to do was find the perfect spot to leave the note he'd written. Q had chosen one he thought would speak of his heart and hint at the fear of rejection he'd been unable to shake. Hopefully, he'd picked the right quote. He hadn't figured out a way to see how Kendall would react. Maybe if he put it on her chair, she'd read it before story time.

Except the moment they walked into the Adventure Cove, the idea flew out the window. Kendall was already sitting in a chair situated in front of the alphabetical carpet. He waved as Deuce ran up to her to give her a hug.

It was one plus in the date-Kendall column. She was one of his son's favorite people. And a testament to what a great person she really was. He didn't know a single kid that came to story time that didn't like Kendall.

He nodded as Daisy walked in with her daughter, Bliss. The two were like carbon copies of one another. Daisy's lighter skin tone matched that of her daughter as did the abundance of curly hair. Only exception was Bliss's hair was lighter and shorter than her mother's.

"Hi, Q. How are you?"

"Good. You?"

"Tired." She smiled as she sat in a chair aligned along the wall, leaving ample sitting room on the floor for the children.

"I hear that. It's amazing how much energy they have."

"No kidding. Not only that but Bliss has been waking up at four each morning."

He shuddered. "That's a pain. Deuce doesn't wake up until seven usually."

"Oh, you're lucky."

Then again, his son never settled down before ten at night, so Q wasn't sure if he was so lucky.

Kendall clapped her hands, gaining the children's attention. "Welcome, you guys. I'm so excited to share some stories today. Can any of you guess what they'll be about?"

"Christmas," a kid shouted.

"No." She shook her head. "Please remember to raise your hands so I can call on you."

Hands shot up in the air. Q chuckled quietly to himself

as Deuce's behind raised up, as if trying to get his hand higher in the air. His son quivered with excitement.

"Deuce?" Kendall called on him.

"Christmas?"

"No. Any other guesses?" She pointed. "Bliss?"

"Fall?"

"Close. We'll be looking at Thanksgiving books." Kendall grabbed a book and told the children a little about the author and illustrator before diving right into the story.

Her voice was melodic, rising up and down as she contorted her voice to mimic the different characters. What would it have been like if his parents had read to him like that? His father had always been a little stoic, hiding his emotions. Q knew his dad loved him, but he rarely said the words. And his mom, well unfortunately, she ran off just like his ex-wife had. There had been no story time. His grandmother had lived in Florida until his grandfather passed and then moved in with his father.

By then, Quinton had been in the military. An adult and in no need for reading unless it had to do with mechanics. When Deuce was born, he'd taken the time to read to his son. It felt awkward at times, like he was making a fool of himself, but the precious sounds of laughter let him know it was worth it. Deuce would know he was loved no matter what.

After three stories, Kendall wrapped up the reading session. She came to her feet, hugging the children and talking to the parents. When she went down a row to help one parent find a book, he walked over to her seat and slipped the note between the stacked children's books she'd left behind.

Lord, I hope this works.

~

Kendall locked the cash drawer. She would balance the receipts in a moment. For now, she wanted to do one last look around before heading to her flat.

"Hey, Kendall," Tiffany said, coming to stand in the doorway. "I was cleaning the Adventure Cove and found this card with your name on it."

Her brow furrowed as she took it. Her name had been written in a loose cursive. If she were a handwriting expert, maybe she could guess the gender of the writer, but she wasn't. "Thanks, Tiff."

"Sure thing. Every room has been straightened up."

"Thanks."

"You're welcome. See you after school tomorrow."

"Have a nice night, sweetie."

Tiffany waved and walked out the front door. Kendall slipped her finger beneath the cream-colored envelope. Who had left her a note and why hadn't they given it to her outright? She smiled at the stationery. It appeared aged, yellow with browned ages. In the middle were the words:

"Stay awhile! 'Tis sweet,. . .
The rare occasion, when our hearts can speak
Our selves unseen, unseeing!"
— Edmond Rostand, author of Cyrano de Bergerac
- Your Secret Admirer

Kendall gasped. Her heart pounded as she read the

words. Could Quinton have had the same idea she'd had? She'd stayed up late last night picking out quotes from different books. Afterward, she'd used her crafting tools to make different scraps of paper that could be quickly added to the gift bags. She had them tucked into a special envelope to ensure Tiffany didn't use them by mistake.

When Q had bought a book for Deuce, she'd slipped one unseen into his bag. Maybe he'd already read his and came back to leave one of his own?

She shook her head. No, he'd only come in once today.

Could it be they were on the same page? Her mind scrolled through the list of patrons, trying to remember if any other males around her age had visited. She frowned. There had been at least three others besides Q. This one card wouldn't be enough to tell if it was him. She'd have to wait and see if he left another or said something about the one she'd slipped in with his purchase.

Lord, please, please let it be Q.

What was it about Quinton Hendricks that had her thinking of moonlit walks and hearts entwined? Sure he was good looking. Cleft chin, check. He appeared to be a great father. Check. He owned his own business. Ambition, check.

But did he like to read? Not just an occasional book once a year. A shudder shook her frame, goosebumps popping up in horror. That would be too awful to contemplate. She wanted to be with an avid reader. She'd learned earlier in life that having no common interests was a huge no-no. Had the divorce decree as proof.

Kendall tapped the note against her palm. If this was from Q, didn't it prove that he was a lover of reading. After all, Cyrano de Bergerac was no light reading, especially if you could read it in French. But not once did she remember Q purchasing a book for himself. His Gran, yes. Deuce, all the time. His father, once in a blue moon. At most, Quinton had an auto mechanic or business magazine in his stack of purchases. She wilted against the wall.

Lord, what will I do if we have nothing in common? All the time I spent searching for the perfect quotes. All the dreams I had.

Well, guess it was proof she needed to pull her head out the proverbial cloud and stay firmly planted in reality. She had to remember what happened when you allowed emotions to sweep you along like a riptide. It was exciting, but one drop from a waterfall and you'd be cautious to dip your toes back in any body of water.

Ty had taught her that.

Charming, good looking, and an appetite for all things classic literature related and Kendall had been sold on his goodness. Two months later, he'd carried her over the threshold and reality had smacked her in the face like a bad book review.

Turned out Ty hated reading anything but classic literature. They'd argued over every modern book that filled her shelves and brought pleasure. Worst of all, he'd held nothing but disdain for her Christian fiction collection. Thought it was an oxymoron and one beneath her intelligence. When a pretty coed agreed, he'd happily left their place for someone worthy of him.

His words, certainly not hers.

Kendall looked down at the note once more. Maybe she should rethink encouraging Quinton. *Lord, what do I do?*

Chapter Five

"She is too fond of books, and it has turned her brain." — Louisa May Alcott, *Work: A Story of Experience*

She liked him, she really liked him. Quinton stared down at the beige slip of paper that he'd found in his bag from The Cozy Shelf.

Q,

Charlotte Brontë said, *"Happiness quite unshared can scarcely be called happiness; it has no taste."*

— Yours truly

There was no name, but it obviously came from Kendall. It had to. His lips slowly curved up into a smile. It had worked. She must have seen his card. Wait, no, that made no sense. This paper looked like it had been crafted. The edges had been cut into a triangle pattern. The quote was written with some kind of glitter pen. And if he wasn't mistaken, she'd somehow added a scent to the paper. He lifted the card to his nose and sniffed. A distinctive floral aroma wafted from it that reminded him of her shampoo.

He had another card ready to go but had to find time to drop it off before going to church. The youth lock-in was tonight. Excitement coursed through him, amping him up. Xavier would be there as well, and the other men's leaders at Heartfalls Community Church were excited to have him on board. Not a single one of them thought he'd be a bad influence. They'd all seen the transformation since Xavier denounced his past and changed who he associated with.

Q grabbed his duffel bag and headed for the living room, where his family sat. His father and grandmother had agreed to watch Deuce. His father would probably get Deuce to help on some car project. And Gran would be the one to tuck him in and read him a book tonight. Q would miss it, but it was only one night. He was just thankful his grandmother wanted to help.

It was moments like this that the absence of his ex-wife seemed to leave a stench behind. Stacy had never been that dependable, but he'd foolishly believed it would change with some vows and a wedding ring. Her normal vivaciousness had seemed to wither away once she'd found out she was pregnant. Even after Deuce was born, she remained a shell of her formal self. Then one day, he'd come home to search for a particular tool only to catch her leaving.

His son had been two months old. Q had thought Deuce would have been inconsolable, but he never seemed to miss the woman who had carried him for nine months.

Shake it off, Q. It's in the past.

Did Kendall have staying power? It was obvious that she liked kids. She did very well with them each story time. Plus, she had ties to the community with running her own business and volunteering at the church. Hopefully, going out with her wouldn't be a mistake like it had been with Stacy.

He said goodbye to his family and headed out the door, his thoughts still trying to pull him back to the past. He needed to refocus, fix his eyes on the One who made life complete. Recalling the words of John 14:27, he repeated them softly to himself. *"Peace I leave with you, My peace I give to you; not as the world gives do I give to you. Let not your heart be troubled, neither let it be afraid."*

A long exhale completed his process of ridding the bad. There was no time to think about Stacy, her absence, or her impact on how he thought about women as a whole. No, he needed to think about the teenagers that would fill the church tonight. Some were at-risk and needed divine intervention stat. Others just wanted to hang out with their friends without their parents hovering over them. Pastor Matt had already assigned groups and leaders to each.

Ten minutes later, he pulled into Heartfalls Community Church. The glass building had a great view of Cayuga Lake and the surrounding greenery. The church had chosen to be a little farther from the heart of the community. It gave them more land to use for recreational activities and outreach programs. Their Autumn Harvest Celebration was a great way to reach those in the community who would otherwise avoid all things church related. And the expansive grounds provided for the perfect backdrop.

Q grabbed his bag and headed inside. Teenagers and their parents were lined up in front of the registration table. Ms. O'Neal smiled and motioned him over.

"Evening, Ms. O'Neal."

"Hey, Q," she beamed, nudging her glasses up on her nose. "We need chaperons to check in and provide their cell number." She pushed the clipboard toward him.

"Got it." He filled out his info and straightened. "Are we still meeting in the pastor's office?"

"Sure are."

"Thanks, Ms. O'Neal."

The pastor's office had already filled with lock-in chaperones. Xavier nodded as Q slipped into the room. Quinton walked around the people and chairs, saying hello, as he made his way toward Xavier. He wanted to make sure his friend didn't have cold feet.

"How's it going Professor?"

"Not bad, man. You ready?"

"Always. I love the lock-ins."

"You know when Deuce gets older, you'll have to bow out."

He chuckled. "Nah, Deuce loves his ol' man."

"That's because he's still young."

Quinton prayed Deuce would always love hanging around him. Hopefully he was fostering that type of relationship.

"Ladies and gentlemen, let's be seated so I can go over the rules."

Before the pastor continued, his office door opened,

and Kendall and Emma Knightley entered. Q's insides tensed up. How had he not known Kendall was a chaperone? Then again, he hadn't seen her when he left the note by the checkout counter. Just a dash in and a drop off.

"Ladies, please have a seat." Pastor Eli looked at the rest of the room. "You should have all checked in with Mrs. O'Neal so that she has your cell number. If you haven't, go see her immediately after we're done here. Our youth pastor Mateo will be leading a sermon and then we'll have break-out sessions. These sessions will be in the groups I've already informed you of. Please lead the kids in the discussion but let them do most of the talking. You're there to make sure the kids are safe and acting appropriately. This doesn't mean to come down on them but to help them along the path they should be going. Please, remember your training."

Q hid a grin. The pastor seemed a little more stressed than usual.

"I'll be on standby if you need me. If not, I'll be enjoying time with the grandkids. This is Mateo's endeavor, so I'm sure he can handle it all. Oh, and one last thing. For those kids who come from a lower income home, please remind them we're putting on a Thanksgiving dinner at the church. All are welcome to attend, but we ask that those eating be in need."

He paused, meeting all of their gazes. "Let's pray."

~

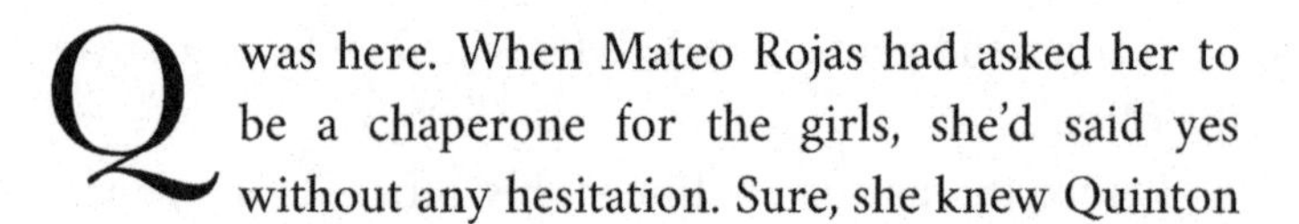

Q was here. When Mateo Rojas had asked her to be a chaperone for the girls, she'd said yes without any hesitation. Sure, she knew Quinton went to Heartfalls Community Church. It wasn't so large that you wouldn't recognize anyone. But she hadn't realized he'd be here as a chaperone.

Was that a sign they had more in common then she'd thought? Kendall glanced to her right and froze. Q's lips curved up in a half-grin that made her stomach flutter. His brown eyes seemed to glow with pleasure.

Because she was here?

She looked away but not before a hint of a smile graced her face. He'd obviously seen the note. Still, she didn't want to come right out and say anything.

Aren't you supposed to pull your head out of the clouds, girl?

But something told her not to. If they had faith in common, couldn't they overcome the many obstacles that life would throw at them? She followed Emma out the door. Now wasn't the time to let her fluttering heart distract her. She was here to help girls like Tiffany. Ones who had a good head on their shoulders but an absent parent or difficult circumstances.

"Earth to Kendall?" Emma called.

"Oops," Kendall lifted her shoulders, spreading her hands as if to say *my bad*.

"No oops. I saw you eyeing Q back there."

"I think he left me a note."

"Are you serious?" Emma stopped, her amber eyes widening.

"Very."

"Did you give him one already?"

Kendall nodded.

"This is so exciting. Maybe you pegged him wrong and he does like literature. Wait, what did it even say?"

"He quoted from Cyrano de Bergac."

Emma grabbed her heart. "I'm happily jealous for you, girl."

"You'll find someone, Em." Kendall laid a hand on her friend's arm.

"Everyone seems to be intimidated by me."

"Why? Because you're gorgeous, have a great job, and a kind heart to boot? More like jealous," Kendall smirked.

"Really?" Emma's face twisted downward.

All her friend wanted was to be seen for who she was inside and not on the outside. More than once, Emma had confided to Kendall about how hard it was to be considered beautiful by the world's standards. Men thought it meant she'd be receptive to their charms and women disliked her for it.

"Look," Kendall said. "That stuff is superficial. Those of us who know you, love you."

"Daisy doesn't."

"I wouldn't say she doesn't love you. She just doesn't know what to do with all those emotions inside."

And boy did Daisy have a lot of emotions. Her parents had given her free rein growing up and it showed at times. Though Daisy had learned to curb her temperament, it could still suck one under.

"I'm glad you love me." Emma hooked her arm through Kendall's.

"Of course. Best friends for life, right?"

"Right. And my job as your bestie is to ensure the romance between you and Q goes smoothly."

"Um...Em?"

"Hmm?"

"Please stay out of it."

"I think I will." Em pointed with her chin.

Kendall turned and stared. Q sidled up toward them, hands in jeans pockets looking perfectly swoon worthy. Seriously, he needed to be in a book.

"Good evening, ladies."

Was it her imagination or did his voice pitch lower? Shivers trailed up her spine as she took a step closer. "Evening, Q." She licked her lips. A nervous habit she couldn't seem to stop. "I didn't know you were volunteering tonight."

"Yes, ma'am." His mouth curved into a half-grin. "I roped one of my friends to help out too."

"Great minds think alike." She pulled Emma to her side, gripping her arm. "You know Emma, right?"

"Of course. Hopefully you'll still be ruling the high school when Deuce gets old enough."

"Time will tell." They shook hands.

"Oh, hey, here comes my friend." Q motioned a lanky man over. "Professor?"

Emma stiffened beside Kendall as a tall drink of water strolled their way. His dark skin gleamed under the recess lighting. He was a little edgy for Kendall's taste, but something told her Emma wasn't thinking that way.

"Ladies, meet my friend Xavier King. Professor, this is Kendall Jackson. She runs The Cozy Shelf."

"We've met." He said in a deep baritone.

"Nice to see you again," Kendall hid a wince as Emma's grip tightened.

"And this is Emma Knightley." Q added. "Our high school principal."

"Nice to meet you." Xavier's gaze switched to her friend.

"Same," Emma squeaked out.

Kendall resisted the urge to stare at her friend. What was up with her?

"Well, we need to meet our group of kids. Talk to you later?"

"Definitely."

A whoosh of air left Emma's body as the men departed.

"What was that?" Kendall placed a hand on her hip, looking at Emma like a bug under a microscope.

"Did you not see him? His eyes were so dark they were like a dreamy onyx color."

Okay. "Did you just revert to a teenager?"

"Kendall, did you *not* see what that man looked like? Why do you think Q called him professor? Does he work at the university?"

"I'm not sure. He buys a lot of nonfiction books with the occasional classic thrown in."

"He reads?" Emma whispered.

Kendall laughed. "We're a sad lot."

"No, my friend. Our life just took an uptick."

Chapter Six

"To be wise and love, Exceeds man's might."— William Shakespeare, *Troilus and Cressida*

"The world is filled with duplicity, deception, and the like. You may find yourself wondering how you can trust what's right in front of you?" Mateo paused, staring out into the crowd.

Q shifted in his seat as the youth pastor continued his sermon.

"This is where trust in God comes in. Proverbs three, verse five teaches us to trust in the Lord with all our heart and lean not on our own understanding." He smiled. A look of mischief crossed his face.

"Do you ever wonder how trust is humanly possible considering the examples of broken trust shoved into our faces on a daily basis? You know when your parents break a promise?"

Chuckles filled the auditorium.

"Or how about when your best friend shares that secret? Or even an advertisement that promised a result you didn't receive?"

Some of the teenagers smirked in recognition.

"If a product doesn't deliver, a social media smear campaign has proven effective. Sometimes even righting wrongs. But what do you do when you believe God has broken your trust?"

A few of the boys in his small group squirmed, unease furrowing their brows. Quinton rested his elbows on his knees. The atmosphere had shifted. Mateo held the teenagers' interest.

"My friends, this is the best time to open the lines of communication. Don't ignore what you're feeling. Don't discount your hurt. Instead, take a page from David. Pour out your hurt in song." The youth pastor pulled out his cell from his back pocket. "Turn to Psalm 22."

He paused a minute before reading. *"My God, My God, why have You forsaken Me?*

Why are You so far from helping Me, And from the words of My groaning? O My God, I cry in the daytime, but You do not hear; And in the night season, and am not silent. But You are holy, enthroned in the praises of Israel. Our fathers trusted in You; They trusted, and You delivered them. They cried to You, and were delivered; They trusted in You, and were not ashamed."

The room hushed. Some people stared into their phones, others their Bibles. At the quietness of Mateo's voice, their attention shifted to the youth pastor.

"David was real in his pain and the Spirit was faithful

to bring into remembrance what God had done for the Israelites. Let us sing."

The teenage worship band began playing. The projector flashed the words *Trust in You by Lauren Daigle.* Q had never heard the song, but the lyrics were powerful as he read them. He looked around at the boys in his group. Some now wore contemplative looks while others remained skeptical. He and Xavier had their work cut out for them. They'd been assigned to six of the young men for the lock-in.

Q bowed his head. *Father, please let Your presence be felt during this lock-in. Please, bless me and the professor with wisdom so we don't lead these young men astray.*

Q peeked to his left, watching as Kendall lifted her hands in worship.

And Lord, I pray that You lead me regarding Kendall. I pray that if it's Your will, she has a permanent place in my future and in Deuce's. I want to be wise in this decision, Father, but I also want the joy of falling in love. To feel that free falling, exhilarating but scary type of love, Lord. And to know that it would be blessed by You. And even better, for Kendall to feel the same way.

And wasn't that the crux of it? He had no idea how she really felt. Sure, she'd left him a note, but did her feelings run as deep as his? Were his feelings even deeper than a liking that made him want to explore a future between them?

Lord, help me know what to say to her and when to say it. Amen.

The song concluded.

Mateo ran back up the auditorium steps to the stage.

"We're going to break into groups right now. Your leaders have been given a list of activities. Please do the first one and then we'll break for dinner."

"Guys, let's stay here." Q pointed to the area they had naturally grouped in.

The first exercise was for a back-to-back drawing. One of the teens would have a pencil and pad and the other would have a picture of what his partner had to draw. Q was excited to see the parallels between their faith and God, as well as the trust it was supposed to inspire.

Xavier set up the chairs, three sets of two back to back. "All right, now pick a partner." Xavier slid his hands into his pockets while the teens grouped up.

"One of you needs to draw and the other needs to be able to describe the picture for your partner."

The boys spoke quietly to themselves, and then each group sat in their spots. Q handed a picture to one of the guys in each pair. "When you're finished, quietly raise a hand. Then I'll share something before you show your partner the finished picture."

The teens began, some eagerly, but soon frustration mounted. Q walked over toward Terrence and Abe. Terrence was erasing his progress. "Start all over, bro. Your directions are whack."

"Man, get outta your feelings. I'm telling you exactly what to draw."

"Chill," Xavier said before Q could jump in. "When your temper rises, it begins to cloud your judgment. Don't give into it. Instead, focus on what he's saying. If you don't get it, ask him to explain another way."

The boys nodded, and Q moved on.

After a while, the three pairs raised their hands. Q glanced at his note card, and then cleared his throat. "All right. You can put your hands down. Did you find the exercise easy?"

"No," they chorused.

"Why?"

Terrence raised his hand.

Q nodded at him.

"I felt like the drawing wasn't going to be right because I didn't know what it was. How could I trust his directions would get me to the right spot?"

"Great question. I've looked at all of your drawings and I can say you all did it correctly. Terrence provided excellent insight to the faith journey."

"What?" Micah exclaimed.

"Think about it." Q folded his arms. "We want God to tell us exactly what our entire journey will look like. We're not satisfied with a direction here or there. What if we wander off the path? Or worse, give up because we believe His directions won't get us to the result we want. What if when we get there, it doesn't look like what we imagined?"

He looked at the boys. "What did you think you were going to draw?"

Jordan raised his hand. "Something complicated. Maybe a car or something I can't draw."

"Exactly. We're afraid no matter how good our skills are, we can't perform." He paused. "What did you draw?"

"A square," the drawers called out.

"And what was the picture you had to tell your partner to draw?"

"A square."

"This is also a portrait of God's grace. He promises to get you to point A. Once you get there, you can trust He'll get you the rest of the way."

Quinton looked at the boys. "All right. Let's eat."

Kendall stared out the bay window facing the lake. She wrapped her arms around her knees, sinking into the plush cushion of the window seat. This week had been slow. Most likely due to people traveling for the Thanksgiving holiday. Emma would be staying in Heartfalls and had invited her to share a Thanksgiving meal. Daisy was traveling to her in-laws for the holiday.

As much as she loved hanging out with Emma, she couldn't muster up the joy of their friendship. All she wanted to do was wallow in pity of being alone. Part of her wanted to rush into Q's arms to avoid the silence and the other side recognized the flaws in her thinking. It was how she'd ended up a divorcee. Forced to watch the man who should have never been her husband find satisfaction elsewhere. If she jumped into a relationship with Q, wouldn't she be repeating the same mistakes?

"Kendall?"

She gulped, and slowly pivoted to face Quinton. He stood with his hands in his jean pockets, which seemed to stretch the material of his gray Henley. How had she missed the subtle muscles in his frame? *You were too busy studying the cleft in his chin.*

Her face heated. "Hey, Q. Do you need help finding something?"

"I..." He rocked back on his heels. "Could you recommend a book for my dad? He wants to read something related to Black history."

"Sure." She unfolded her legs and stood.

Her equilibrium tilted, and Kendall told herself it had nothing to do with the man of her dreams standing in front of her with a look of caution on his face. It was like neither one of them knew how to act now that the first notes had been exchanged. Maybe if she slipped another one into his bag their relationship would right itself.

Her mind filtered through the quotes she'd written down, praying for the perfect one to indicate her feelings...and perhaps a little of her fear.

"Do you know what era of history he wants?"

"Not really."

"Does he read a lot or only here and there?" She needed to know if a big book would intimidate him.

"Oh, he's usually reading something. I know he's read about the Civil Rights leaders."

"That helps."

She headed for The Study which housed all the nonfiction works. "How big are the books he usually reads?"

"Pretty thick."

"I always say the longer the book, the better."

Q chuckled. "I believe it." He nodded at her. "Your shirts are always the best. Makes me wish I could wear ones with automobiles on it instead of the jumpsuit we have."

Kendall paused in the doorway, looking up at Q. "But isn't it comfortable? I always imagined it was like wearing pajamas."

"Yeah but the material isn't that soft, not like a cotton tee would be."

Were they really talking about clothes? Kendall searched her feelings, and decided she didn't care. This was the most they'd talked about something involving him.

"Well that Henley looks comfortable." She wanted to snuggle in his arms and feel it.

Down, girl. She stepped into the room. *Must focus.* "How about The Warmth of Other Suns? It's about the Great Migration in the African-American community."

"I've never seen him read anything like it. Sounds good."

Kendall crossed her arms, leaning against the bookshelf. "What are you getting Deuce for Christmas?"

"I don't know," he mumbled, rubbing a hand across his chin.

The one she'd kiss if she were his girlfriend. *Think books, Kendall.* "Maybe books?"

"Deuce loves bedtime because I'll read him a story. But I doubt he wants me to buy him books for Christmas."

Good point. "A bike? Do they still make Big Wheels?"

"They do."

"Maybe a set of cars he can build." She'd seen a commercial for that on Netflix the other night.

"I like that." His lips inched up with pleasure. "Thank you."

"Sure." She pointed to the book in his hand. "You ready to pay?"

"Yes."

She headed toward the stairs, conscious of Q's movements behind her. The sound of his boots as they took the steps down one at a time sent a thrill through her. What would it be like if she stopped and let her hand touch his?

Ugh. It was all so reminiscent of her romance with Ty. Her feelings had rushed ahead, spinning a life of forever in her mind before they even went out on a date. After a month, she'd word vomited her feelings on love. Two months after their first date, she'd sealed her fate in front of a justice of the peace.

"Not this time," she whispered.

"What?"

Kendall startled, arms flailing as she sought to right herself. Capable hands reached out to steady her by her waist. The warmth from his palms seared through her *Book Nerd* t-shirt. How had she forgotten Q was behind her?

"You okay?"

The low tone touched her like a caress. The hairs on the back of her neck stood. "Yes," she breathed.

She straightened to her full height of five feet six inches and pivoted on her heels to face Q. "I appreciate that."

"Any time." His Adam's apple bobbed. "Kendall, I..."

"Yes?" She leaned forward.

"Never mind." He held the book out. "I should buy this. My lunch break is almost over, and I still need to grab a sub."

"Right." She blinked and rushed to the checkout counter.

She scanned his book, and then grabbed a plastic bag. Without a thought, she grabbed the first slip from the hidden compartment and placed it into the bag. Hopefully, it was true to her heart and not mortifyingly embarrassing.

"Have a good day, Q."

"You too, Kendall."

Chapter Seven

"Let us never underestimate the power of a well-written letter."
—Jane Austen, *Persuasion*

Quinton settled down into his Adirondack chair, letting the peaceful quiet of the night close around him. Kendall's slip of paper had burned a hole in his back pocket all day, calling to him. But he couldn't bring himself to pull it out and read it.

Too afraid of what it might say.

Stop bothering me?

Oops, that note was for someone else?

Or worse: *did you think you were the only one getting these?*

Of course, his mind had spun a tale for every rejection imaginable. He hated how much the divorce had changed him. Gone were the confident thoughts of a man who knew the plans God have for him. A wife, a family, and a job creating a legacy that his father had started. Now one little slip of paper had his mind spinning out of control with doubts plaguing him.

A chill in the air reminded him winter would soon descend in all its glory.

Quinton slipped his fingers into his back pocket and pulled the folded paper out. *Lord, however this goes, please guide me in my response and next steps. Amen.* With that, he opened the craft paper.

Q,

From the words of William Shakespeare, *"A heart to love, and in that heart, Courage, to make's love known."*

– Yours truly

Courage. The irony pulled a chuckle from his lips. The notes were supposed to bolster him. Instead, with each one, his insides twisted more than if he took the risk to ask Kendall out. But now he knew she was essentially saying the same thing. She needed courage as well.

What lay in her past to make her hesitant?

"Lord, help." He laid back against the chair, letting it take the pressure of his lower back. His shoulders slumped as he thought about all the ins and outs of dating. Dating as a single father. As a business owner. As one whose time already felt split into too many strands. What made him think he could give more?

"Two are better than one, because they have a good reward for their labor."

The words of Ecclesiastes flashed in his mind. At the end of the day, he really had no one to share his life with. Yes, his father and grandmother walked alongside him, but his dad was more focused on taking care of his grandmother. And the father-son relationship he had with Deuce was worlds apart from that of a husband and wife.

He crossed his feet at the ankles, shifting his arms up over his head to rest against his interlaced fingers.

"Something bothering you, Quinton?"

He peered over his shoulder and shrugged. "Life's difficult sometimes, Dad."

"Ain't that the truth." His father sat in the empty chair, placing his hands over his stomach. "What's taking up the attic space?"

Q's lips quirked at the old saying his grandmother was always throwing around. She said it whenever she thought they were thinking too hard. "Just pondering whether entering into another relationship is worth all the potential heartache."

"That certainly is worth your thoughts."

"You don't think I'm overthinking?"

"You have to. You have Deuce."

"Yeah," he sighed. "Why didn't you ever remarry?"

"I thought about it. Met a woman or two who caught my interest. But in the end, I didn't feel that tug or the desire to go further. When I prayed about it, I always had the sense that my life was the way it should be. I had you to look after, a shop to run, and then your grandmother came to live with us."

"Did you ever feel like something was missing?"

"Not once. Do you?"

"Often." Q stared straight ahead. It was a little uncomfortable sharing, but he really wanted his father's thoughts on the matter.

"Then sounds like you need to investigate it."

"But what if something happens? What if it doesn't work? I don't want to introduce a woman into Deuce's life for him to get attached, and then she doesn't stick around." He shook his head.

"But what if it does work out? Hmm?"

Then Kendall would be the one sitting out here with me.

Goosebumps trailed down his arms. He could perfectly imagine her here, in his home, sitting with him at church, and joining him for Deuce's bedtime stories.

"I take your silence to mean the idea appeals."

"It does."

"Then go for it. Is it Kendall?"

He snorted. "I'm that obvious?"

"I don't know how others see you, but you're my son. You've been on this earth thirty-five years now. I'm sure all that time with you helped clue me in." His dad winked.

"It worked."

"Well you won't know if the lady likes you until you ask her out."

"I kind of already put feelers out." He faced his dad.

His father's eyebrow cocked. "How'd you do that?"

"Wrote her a note but left off my signature."

"How is she supposed to know you sent it?"

"She sent me one back." His hand froze before he could hand over the slip of paper. Something told him to keep the words between him and Kendall private.

"Then go for it. Stop worrying you'll get hurt again. Don't let Stacy's actions dictate your future."

Q frowned. "How can I not?"

"Easy. It's in the past."

There was a time that would have hurt like a boxer's left hook. Instead he nodded in agreement. Stacy no longer wanted to be a part of his life. She made that clear when she abandoned Deuce and later when she sent divorce papers. He hadn't heard from her since, and she'd made no move to visit Deuce.

He'd always wanted to be married, and maybe that had prompted his rushed relationship with his ex. Shouldn't he take the time to figure out how to navigate through a relationship on God's timing. But how?

Kendall stooped over to double tie her boots. Her mind wondered to Quinton and his thoughts on her quote. Would he have the courage to ask her out? Would she have the courage to say yes?

She sighed while stretching her arms to the heavens. A hike around Heartfalls State Park should clear her mind and right her thoughts. Being out in nature always made her think of God's great majesty and the comfort of being His. It was the perfect way to unwind after an early morning at church.

The crisp fall air beckoned to her, promising her perfect scenery to stimulate her mind and rejuvenate her soul. She glanced at her wristwatch. It had an open face of a book, surrounded by quartz and a red leather band. *11:00 am.*

Daisy and Emma should be here soon. They had both agreed to hike with her and to keep their negative comments about one another to themselves.

Father, if You could give some divine wisdom on how to get those two to get along, it would be much appreciated.

From the first day of their literature class, Kendall had

known she would be friends with Daisy and Emma. Unfortunately, they didn't pick up the memo and had disliked one another on sight. She couldn't understand it because they were both wonderful women.

The sound of tires on gravel reached her ears. Kendall glanced at the parking entrance and smiled when she saw Emma's car, quickly followed by Daisy's minivan. The two parked and walked toward her, not a word exchanged between the two of them.

Please let them behave, Lord.

Kendall wrapped Emma in a hug before doing the same with Daisy. "Hey, ladies."

"Hi."

"Hey, girl," Emma said. Her long hair had been pulled into a ponytail, accenting her almond shaped eyes and flawless skin.

Daisy had all her curls pulled into a blue-and-white crocheted slouch beanie big enough to fit over all her hair. Kendall had a similar red-and-white one, but it was a lot smaller considering the small afro puff of hair that she usually pulled on top of her head.

"Ready?"

They nodded.

Kendall led the way, crossing the small footbridge to the hiking trail. "How's life treating you, Daisy?"

She frowned, her pert nose scrunching with concern. "Bliss smashed her finger in the porch screen a few minutes before I left."

"Oh no," Emma exclaimed.

Bliss had sickle cell anemia and a smashed finger could lead to worse problems.

"Is she okay?" Kendall paused to search her friend's face.

"She crawled into Sean's lap, and he was able to rock her to sleep. He promised to call if there was a problem." Daisy held up her cell phone.

"Should we pray?" Emma asked.

Even though they didn't get along, at least Kendall's two best friends would pray for one another. It gave her hope that they could one day forge a friendship.

"Please," Daisy whispered.

Kendall bowed her head. "Father, we ask that You bring healing to Bliss. Please put a hedge of protection around her. Please boost her immune system and keep her from getting a pain crisis or any other sickle cell complications." She paused, searching for the right words.

"And Lord," Emma joined in. "We ask that You give Daisy and Sean wisdom to know if Bliss needs medical attention. Please strengthen them and bring peace to their fears."

"Amen," Daisy whispered.

"Amen," Kendall and Emma repeated.

Their steps took them along the trail, but silence had descended upon their group. Bliss had already suffered so much in her four years on this earth. At one time, Daisy had moved away from Heartfalls for a year in hopes warmer temperatures would help Bliss. Unfortunately, the higher temperatures hadn't been an improvement to her health either.

When Daisy first told her about Bliss's diagnosis, Kendall had scoured the internet for all information related to sickle cell. The little girl had a lesser variant, but from where Kendall stood, it wasn't any easier. She'd already had her spleen removed and usually had at least one hospitalization a year. It was heart breaking, but Bliss was a strong kid. Always smiling, always giggling.

On healthy days, that is.

Kendall turned her attention to her friends. "How's everything with you, Em?"

"Good. A little quiet now that the holiday break is here. I'm really looking forward to Christmas break. There's just something about that two-week period that rejuvenates me."

"It's the beauty of Christmas." Kendall smiled. "I think I'll decorate The Cozy Shelf this weekend."

"Oh fun!" Daisy clapped her hands, concern melting away to excitement. "Do you need help?"

"Definitely. Some of the higher places are a little difficult to reach."

"Maybe your *friend* should help you." Emma waggled her eyebrows, drawing laughter from Daisy.

Kendall didn't know whether to smile in amusement or run from their good-natured ribbing.

"That's a fantastic idea," Daisy said. "You guys can decorate every floor together and let your attraction bloom and voila." She spread her hands out.

"Voila indeed," Emma replied. "Any updates on the note exchange?"

"Nothing yet." Not that she expected to hear anything today. The shop was never open on Sundays.

"He'll probably stop by first thing tomorrow." Daisy offered.

"I'm trying not to think about it, honestly. All I know is I want to have the courage to say yes if he asks me out."

"But why wouldn't you?" Daisy stopped walking,

looking at Kendall as if she'd sprouted an unsightly wart on her nose.

"Whirlwind romances don't work."

"I beg to differ." Daisy crossed her arms, her jaw tightening.

Kendall winced. "Okay, there are exceptions. But I'm not one. Don't you remember?"

"That was Ty's fault, not yours." Emma pursed her lips.

"I'm not talking about the cheating. You have to admit, we jumped into a relationship awfully fast."

"I'll admit no such thing." Daisy said. She kicked at a rock, and then continued walking up the hill. "Let's keep going."

They trudged up the small incline. Silence fell between them, and Kendall soaked it all in. The soft rustling of the remaining leaves. The chirping of the birds. As they continued on the path, the sound of the waterfall began to reach her ears. The smell in the air changed, bringing a freshness. The sound of the water cascading over the rocks greeted them.

Kendall stopped, leaning on the viewing rail and taking in the picturesque scene. How had He done it? If she were in the water, the fear of falling down the waterfall would overwhelm her. Yet watching the scene was as peaceful as a bubbling brook. It was like God showing His majesty and gentleness all at the same time.

"I love it here," Emma whispered.

"Me too." Kendall and Daisy spoke simultaneously, exchanging smiles as their voices blended to one.

"It reminds me that nothing is too hard for God." Kendall added.

"Most definitely." Daisy nodded. She paused as her cell's ringtone rent the tranquility of the moment.

Kendall bit her lip. Was it Bliss? She watched as Daisy retreated, a finger in one ear, cell against the other.

"Do you think Bliss will have to go to the hospital?" Emma asked as she sidled up next to Kendall.

"I hope not. That cutie has had enough of the hospital to last a lifetime."

"Unfortunately, that's her future."

Suddenly, Kendall wondered why she was afraid to let Quinton know why he mattered to her. If Bliss could face down illness at four years of age, couldn't Kendall tell Quinton how much she liked him?

Chapter Eight

""The dearest ones of time, the strongest friends of the soul--
BOOKS." — Emily Dickinson

Quinton climbed the steps to the second floor of Kendall's bookstore. Her absence on the first floor had become evident after going in and out of each room. He'd awakened this morning intent on asking her out. After much prayer last night, he realized the only thing preventing him from going forward was himself. God certainly hadn't placed any limitations on his desire to have a relationship with her. It was his own doing. His own fears keeping him prisoner.

A quick glance in the Adventure Cove told him no one was in the room. He walked over to the Masterpiece Corner and stilled. The cozy winter's night scent was back. The one that reminded him of warmed sugar. He stepped over the threshold. Should he call out for her? *No.*

He paused at the third row of bookshelves. There she stood, holding an open book, a pair of black-rimmed eyeglasses perched on her nose. He smiled and leaned against the shelf.

"I had no idea you wore glasses."

Slowly, she looked up and met his gaze. "Afternoon, Q."

"Good afternoon to you too, Kendall."

Her tongue darted out, licking her lips then retreating. "Did you need something?"

You. He gulped. "I..."

"Actually," she straightened. "Maybe you could help me out?"

"Sure." *Anything.*

"Could you help me decorate? I usually do it the day after Thanksgiving, but if you and your family already have plans, I could do it a different day."

"No, Friday's perfect." He paused. It wasn't a date, but maybe that fear creeping up his spine would be gone by then. *She isn't Stacy.* He needed to keep reminding himself of that.

"Great." Her brown eyes lit up.

The contrast of her dark colored eyes and light brown skin captivated him. He wanted to draw closer and take her all in.

"How's nine?"

Her words jolted him to reality. "Oh, that should be fine. Deuce will be awake by then, so I can tell him I'm leaving. He likes to know where I am."

Apparently, he wasn't the only one dealing with abandonment issues.

"You're welcome to bring him."

Even though it wasn't a date, Q didn't want Deuce with him. Who knows, maybe it would lead to something. "Thanks, but it'll probably be better if my grandmother watches him. That way if any of your ornaments are glass, he won't be tempted to break something."

She chuckled. "Okay."

"I'll see you then?"

"Yes."

He walked out the room and back down the stairs. Pausing, Q took in the mug shelf. Kendall always used the mug that read *Please go away, I'm reading.* He took the note he'd brought, just in case courage failed him, out of his jacket pocket and slid it behind the mug. Hopefully she wouldn't mind waiting a little longer for an invitation to dinner since today's attempt had obviously not gone according to plan.

The bell jingled, and Quinton straightened, peering at the door. The youth pastor walked through the door.

"Hey, Q."

"Morning, Pastor."

"How many times have I asked you to call me Matt? Save the title for Pastor Eli."

Q nodded as they shook hands. "That was an amazing lock-in last weekend."

"It was." Matt folded his arms and rested his chin in the V between his finger and thumb. "I had lots of the teens coming up to talk to me afterward. A few from your group of guys."

"To God be the glory, man. Some of those kids have had a tough life."

"No doubt, but now they know they aren't alone."

"You do a good job of that, P— I mean, Matt."

Matt chuckled. "I try, my friend. It's difficult. Most of the kids assume I have some cushy life because I have a title in front of my name. But the lock-in provided an opportunity to share about my background."

Q nodded. It had been an inspiring testimony. Matt's parents had immigrated from Colombia to offer him a better life. They'd lived in a one-bedroom apartment, Matt sharing the living room couch with his younger brother. Matt wouldn't have escaped the gangs in his neighborhood if it weren't for the wisdom of his father and local church. He wanted to show others there was another way.

"What are you doing here? Buying something for Deuce?" Matt asked, quirking his head to the side.

Q's face heated. "Uh..."

Matt laughed, clamping a hand on Q's shoulder. "Didn't mean to put you on the spot. You're looking a little red in the face."

The door chimed, and Daisy rushed in. Her eyes were widened, panic flitting her eyes back and forth. "Where's Kendall?"

"Upstairs." Q motioned behind him. "Masterpiece Corner."

"Thanks." Her feet pounded up the stairs.

"Should we pray?" Matt asked.

"Seems like it."

They bowed their head.

"Heavenly Father, we come to You on behalf of Daisy. Lord, may Your peace flood her heart and may Your strength calm her storms. Whatever we can do, may we be obedient to do so and ease our sister's burden. In Jesus' name, Amen."

"Amen." Q looked at the pastor. "Xavier is coming over for Thanksgiving. Would you like to join us?"

"That would be my pleasure. My brother is flying our parents down to California for the holidays to be with his family. Thank you."

"Anytime. I need to head out, but I'll text you my address."

"Thanks again."

Q jogged down the bookstore steps and headed to his car. The visit didn't turn out like he'd imagined, but that was okay. Matt would be able to enjoy the holidays with some friends. He stared up into the second-floor windows. He hoped everything was okay in there.

Lord, let it be so.

~

"Kendall?" Daisy called out.

She walked to the edge of the row to meet Daisy. Kendall's stomach twisted when she saw the look on Daisy's face. "Is something wrong with Bliss?"

"No," she waved a hand in the air. "She's good."

Thank You. Kendall sagged against the bookshelf. Her friend began pacing back and forth and Kendall straightened. A crisis hadn't been averted after all. "What's wrong?"

"Paula's here."

"What?" Kendall walked closer to Daisy. To what? Give her a hug?

"Yes, she arrived late last night. Didn't get a hotel. Didn't even ask if I minded if she could visit."

"Well, she is your sister."

"Half," Daisy snapped, curls whipping her face.

Tread softly, Kendall. Daisy had a lot of history with her parents. They had split when she was a toddler. Daisy had stayed with her mom. And her father had started a new life, adding another daughter almost two years later.

"Did you see if the hotels had any openings?"

"They don't," she snorted. "Why would anything go my way when Paula shows up? The universe is out to get me."

"Daisy." Kendall led her friend to the window seat. "Breathe. You know that's not how life works. The universe isn't out to get you. God has you."

Daisy rubbed the middle of her forehead. "I'm sorry. My emotions got the best of me and my mom's mumbo jumbo came out."

"It's okay. Maybe this is the perfect time to bridge the gap with Paula. Maybe you can become friends."

"Really?" If the curl of Daisy's lip hadn't been indication enough of her feelings, the disdain dripping from her words got the message across.

Kendall sat back as her brain silently counted to ten. Daisy was hurting right now and clearly not thinking of their friendship. She would have to remember for the both of them. "Daisy, do you want me to pray for you?"

"No."

Kendall's eyebrows shot up. "Daisy, girl."

"Fine." She turned toward Kendall before closing her eyes.

"Lord God, please help Daisy. Please bring her peace and calm. Please show her what You want her to learn out of this situation. Please help her find some common ground with Paula, Lord. And please slow her anger. In Jesus' name, Amen."

"Amen." A tear slid down Daisy's cheek. "I'm sorry for being so awful, Kendall."

"I know you're hurting." She wrapped her arms around Daisy. "It's going to be all right, okay?"

Daisy's head bobbed up and down as she continued to squeeze Kendall. "I don't want to come in second place any longer."

"And you don't." Kendall pulled back to look at her friend. "You have a little girl who looks up to you. Who knows she means the world to you and Sean. Look at the life you've created, not the one you were raised in."

Daisy wiped her face with her hands. "You're right."

"Of course I am." She winked. "Want to go downstairs and get some coffee and a muffin?"

"Not if Q and the pastor are still down there. I look a hot mess."

"Q didn't leave?" Kendall leaned to the left, trying to hear the sounds downstairs.

"You could always go downstairs and look, Kendall." Daisy chuckled and shook her head.

"True. And if the pastor is here, then I should go see if he needs something or is ready to purchase."

"It's not Pastor Eli." Daisy twisted her mouth to the side. "It's the youth pastor."

"Oh, Matt. He probably wants to know if his order came in."

Kendall led the way out the room. As she stepped onto the first floor, her heart sunk. Q was nowhere to be found.

"*Holá,* Kendall," A boyish grin lit Matt's face.

"*Holá,* Mateo." She greeted the pastor in Spanish, thankful she had the opportunity to use her high school elective. She hated for knowledge to go to waste. "Your package arrived late yesterday."

"Great. I had some free time and thought I'd check."

Kendall went into the checkout room and looked under the counter where she left the stack of Romans' Bible studies.

"See you later, Kendall," Daisy called from the doorway.

"Chin up, okay?"

Daisy nodded and gave a little wave before disappearing from sight.

"Everything okay?" Matt asked.

"It will be." She passed the bag of books to him. "Was Q here when you walked in?"

"Yeah. He left soon after Daisy walked in."

"Oh."

"Everything okay?"

Her face heated under his scrutiny. "Yes."

"I'll talk to you later then."

"*Adiós.*"

Kendall couldn't wait to put her feet up and rest. Today had been relatively quiet but every time she got ready to open a book of her own, someone showed up. Poor Daisy was a mess. She could only pray her friend didn't let her temper get the better of her. Not that she minded her friend coming to her for aid. And she especially enjoyed seeing Q again.

"Wait," she whispered. Had he left a note somewhere in the store? He hadn't bought anything so why had he come in?

She looked around the counter, but nothing appeared out of place. She strolled toward the hospitality table, noting with surprise the amount of money stuffed into the tip jar. But it couldn't hold her attention, not when a blue envelope beckoned behind her coffee mug. She smiled as she slid it out of the cubby.

Inhaling, Kendall breathed in the light, airy scent with a touch of motor oil clinging to the envelope. Q. Her lips curved upward. The man had no idea what he did to her. She opened the envelope and pulled out the simple black-lined paper.

"You have been the last dream of my soul."
— Charles Dickens, *A Tale of Two Cities*

"Oh, Q," she whispered.

Chapter Nine

"I will honor Christmas in my heart, and try to keep it all the year." — Charles Dickens

Whispering a prayer, Quinton knocked on the door of The Cozy Shelf. It didn't seem as well-lit as usual. Kendall had texted him to stop by at nine this morning. Maybe she had overslept trying to sleep off the pounds gained from yesterday's turkey fest. He knew he added some weight around the middle. His gran had been intent on plying the men with food before retiring to watch Thanksgiving movies.

Just as he was about to knock again, the door swung open.

Kendall smiled at him, her pink lips parting, giving him a flash of straight white teeth. Her hair had been pulled into an Afro puff on the top of her head. She looked adorable despite the horrendous reindeer sweater she wore.

"Morning, Q." She stepped back and motioned for him to enter.

"Morning." He slid his hands into his pockets as she re-locked the front doors.

"Do you need some coffee?" She pointed to the hospitality table and then shook her head, looking sheepish.

It sat empty.

She cleared her throat. "I actually have some coffee at my place upstairs."

"No, that's okay. I don't drink it."

"Ever?"

He chuckled. "Never."

"Why?" she asked in a shock whisper.

"Gives me a stomach ache."

"Oh, that's a bummer."

Quinton shrugged. He didn't like the taste of it either, but perhaps one little unveiling at a time would be best. "So what's the plan here?"

"Deck the shelves until the store gleams with Christmas cheer." She leaned forward, her cheeks bunched with excitement. "Can you tell it's my favorite time of year?"

He held his thumb and pointer close together. "Just a smidge."

She gave him a sparkling grin.

His fingers itched to pull her close and kiss her. She'd never looked more desirable than she did at this moment. Eyes brimming with joy, cheeks flushed with pleasure.

"Come on," she motioned for him to follow. Kendall walked up the stairs. "I got tired dragging the totes, so I stopped on the second floor." She pointed. "There are more outside my apartment."

"Kendall." He cocked an eyebrow while shaking his head. Two full-size rectangular totes sat on the landing. "How many are upstairs?"

"Two more."

"Not bad."

"For you." She snorted. "You can probably lift one with your man muscles and be fine. I'm dying from the effort of sliding them down the stairs."

Man muscles? She was adorable. *Lord, help me keep my cool and my lips to myself.* "Do both of these need to go to the first floor or can one of them stay here?"

Her lips twisted in thought. "Let's see." She popped the first tote open, peeking through the contents. "This one can go downstairs. I know the perfect places for the decorations."

"Great." He lifted the tote. "Be right back."

With Kendall's direction, he moved the remaining totes to the appropriate floors before meeting her near the front of the store. Kendall wanted the main floor to be ready first in case they ran out of steam and couldn't make it to the others. It was a sound plan.

"Let's decorate the tree." Kendall clapped her hands, rubbing them together with glee.

Q chuckled. "You're too much."

"No way. One can't be too excited about Christmas." She stopped and stared at him. "Have you seen *The Man Who Invented Christmas?*"

"No. Is it good?"

"The best." She sighed. "Nothing could be better than books and Christmas put together."

"I take it you like this whole book world you've created?" He motioned around him.

She placed a hand on her hip, tilting her head to the side in exasperation. "You did not just ask me that ridiculous question."

His chest rumbled with suppressed laughter. "Just wanted to see what you would do."

"Right," she drew out. Kendall bit her lip and stared at him for a moment. Just before discomfort could set in, she spoke. "Do you read?"

"Every day. I have to read receipts, prices at the grocery store—

She threw a plastic book ornament at him. "Seriously."

"Sorry." He held his hands up in mock surrender. "I read to Deuce every night unless I'm not home for whatever reason. Of course, you know of my magazine habit."

"I do. But I'm talking about books. Non-fiction, fiction, etc."

"Does the Bible count?"

She stared at him, biting her pink lip again.

A band of worry squeezed his chest. Was this a roadblock for her? "Kendall?"

"I don't like repeating mistakes."

"Understand." *Not really.* Well, he understood, but didn't see how the two correlated.

"I knew someone who didn't like to read anything but classic literature. It was a problem for us."

"And you think me just reading children's books and magazines will be a problem for..." He trailed off, letting the understood *us* float in the air.

"It could be, couldn't it?" Her worried eyes met his.

"Or it could not be. I don't have a problem with a

person who reads. I want Deuce to be a man who reads. I just don't make time to do so myself. Too busy with the business and being a dad, I guess."

"Do you watch TV?"

"Not really. I'm more of a movies kind of guy when I have the time. Unless, of course, the TV is playing a ball game."

The worry faded away. "What kind of movies?"

"I'll watch anything once, but I prefer action and comedies."

"Have you ever seen Pride and Prejudice?"

"No. Is it a drama?"

She guffawed, bending at the waist. Her laughter infectious, Q found himself grinning along even though he knew he was the butt of the joke.

"It's a period drama, but it's also a romance." She gasped as if trying to muffle laughter behind his blunder.

"I'd watch it once."

A gleam entered her brown eyes. "How much time do you have?"

Kendall couldn't believe it. She snuck a glance at Quinton out of the corner of her eye. His eyes were trained on her TV as Mr. Darcy declared the state of his unchanged feelings. She'd chosen to watch the Kiera Knightley version of *Pride and Prejudice* since Q had a little boy to get home to and decorating The Cozy Shelf had already taken a couple of hours. Otherwise, the BBC version would be in her DVD player stat.

Thankfully, this version wasn't her favorite because

she'd been too busy noticing the man beside her instead of the one on screen. She'd been hyperaware of Q from the moment he sat down on her love seat. Kendall had tried to shrink her frame, curling her legs underneath her and leaning toward the arm of the sofa, but the smell of his cologne caressed her face with each movement of his body. One moment he had an arm on the back of the sofa, begging for her to hold it or lean her face against it.

Then he'd change directions.

It was maddening and awfully distracting. But as the movie began to wind down, she refocused. She couldn't let the last kiss go unseen by glancing at Q's profile. Kendall turned her eyes to the screen, soaking in the music notes, the joy on Lizzy and Mr. Darcy's faces.

The credits started rolling, and she released a pent-up breath. "So, what did you think?" She turned her body to face Q. *Huh, there's more space between us now.* And the cold that lingered at the widening gap kind of depressed her.

"I think I'm happy the movie wasn't longer."

She chuckled. "Then be happy I didn't have you watch my favorite version."

"It wasn't terrible," he hedged. "But not something I'd watch again."

"We could watch the Bollywood version next time?" She tried to hide a grin.

He blinked slowly. Once. Twice. "I don't even know what to say to that, Kendall."

She gulped, a shiver of awareness tingling her spine at the sound of her name on his lips. "Say yes?"

"I think it's my turn to choose the movie. However, it'll have to wait until next time."

Her heartbeat sped up. *There would be another time?* "All right. Sounds like a plan."

"Great." He flashed a grin, and her insides melted.

Now she felt like Emma, reverting back to a teenager with a crush on the hot guy at school. Except Q was the hot mechanic sitting on her sofa. She pinched the inside of her wrist.

Quinton stood. "I need to go. I promised Deuce we'd play trains and eat popcorn."

"Of course." She rose to her feet. "Tell him thanks for letting you hang with me today. I know everyone's going to love the decorations when the store opens again."

"It was my pleasure."

She intertwined her fingers, resting her chin on them to prevent her from reaching out and grabbing him up in a hug. *Go slowly. Don't let your feelings take over.*

"I'll walk you downstairs."

The sounds of their footsteps seemed to echo as they worked down the winding staircase now covered in ivy. The white lights entwined in the greenery sparkled in the darkness. Kendall didn't want to see him go, but she desperately needed to take things slower. If only to show herself that she wouldn't be the same foolish twenty-year-old jumping into the first relationship offered to her.

"Thanks again, Q." She stood in front of The Cozy Shelf's door, where the bookish wreath had been hung.

"Any time, Kendall." He gazed into her eyes and then his eyes travelled upward.

Her own followed his track and she froze, staring at the mistletoe he'd hung earlier. Her gaze flew to his and her cheeks heated.

"See you later, Kendall," he whispered softly. He leaned forward achingly slow and placed a kiss on her cheek.

Her eyes closed, soaking in the feel of his warm, soft lips. His chin stubble caressed her face softly, sending cheers of awareness up her arms. The pressure of his mouth lightened as he drew away. She let go of the door knob and moved out of his way.

Could he hear the beat of her heart?

She watched as he walked down the steps. His truck parked along the curb looked lonely under the street lights. Q waved a hand and then opened his door, disappearing from view. Kendall let out a pent-up sigh and closed the door.

"Best time ever, Lord."

Her fingers wiggled as the urge to dial Emma or Daisy and tell them about her day swelled within her. But then again, maybe she should just treasure the sweet moment and relive it over and over in her mind. She glanced up at the mistletoe. "Thank you for that wonderful kiss."

Chapter Ten

"But for my own part, if a book is well written, I always find it too short." —Jane Austen

Quinton closed the book and looked down at his son. "What did you think of the story?"

"It was too short. Can you read it again?"

Deuce said the same thing whenever Q read an *Elephant and Piggie* book. Quinton had to admit, the duo was highly amusing. Plus, Deuce got a kick out of his idea of what the two sounded like. It was a requirement that any book he read to his son be done with different voices for each character.

"Not tonight. We're going to get our Christmas tree tomorrow, remember?"

Deuce's brown eyes widened. "Right," he whispered. "Night, Daddy."

"Night, Deuce."

Q laid a kiss on his son's forehead and headed for the door. He paused, pressing the button on the dinosaur-shaped night light. Leaving the door open a crack, he walked to his room, right next door to Deuce's. His grandmother had the master, and his father had renovated the sunroom into a bedroom for himself.

Q slipped inside his bedroom and let out a sigh. Today had been a long day but one with many rewards. He flopped backwards onto his bed, sinking into the memory-foam-topped mattress. It welcomed his body, molding to his shape and taking the aches away. He let out a sigh as an image of Kendall sprang to mind.

Spending the day with her had been one of the best things he'd done in the last few years. Her warm laughter had wrapped itself around his heart. He hadn't been sure about his feelings before spending time with her, but now he knew. Kendall could have him shopping for rings and imagining a different life than the one he currently had.

One that held the mixture of a family's laughter. He closed his eyes, imagining himself around a Christmas tree with Deuce and Kendall. Not just for the foreseeable future, but one that continued until their family grew along with the gray on their heads. Thoughts of what-could-be followed him until he fell asleep.

"Daddy, wake up! It's Saturday."

Q wrestled one eye open and flinched at the closeness of his son's face. He should probably be thankful Deuce wasn't peeling his eyelids back. "I'm awake," he mumbled, voice scratchy with sleep.

"Then get up, Daddy." Deuce tugged at his arms, trying to pull him into a sitting situation.

Lord, help. Q sighed. Mornings weren't his favorite things, especially when a little person was trying to wake him up earlier than he wanted. Quinton rolled to his side and propped himself up on an elbow while rubbing sleep from his eyes.

"Gran's making pancakes."

"Okay. I'll be there in a minute."

"Yay!" Deuce ran from the room, excitement elevating his voice to dog whistle proportions.

Q winced and stood as his back cracked with a stretch. He grabbed his cell phone and opened his Bible app, looking at the verse of the day.

"Thanks be to God for His indescribable gift!" – 2 Corinthians 9:15 NKJV

Thank You, Lord, for reshifting my focus. May I never forget the gift of salvation. May I never forget the gift of waking up each day or having my son look up to me. I know that time will change. May I treasure each moment instead of grumbling.

He glanced back at his bed. *And it's so hard not to complain. My bed is really soft. But I know You'll correct me when I get off course or too close to the line. Thank You, Lord. Please bless this day with my family.*

Q shook his head and rubbed his chin. He had a little extra facial hair this morning, but nothing that would have him running for his trimmers. A quick shower should do the trick. By the time he made it to the breakfast table, his son was practically bouncing in his seat.

"Eat your pancakes, Deuce."

"I am," he mumbled around food.

"Don't talk with your mouth full, Deuce."

His son sighed, slapping a hand to his forehead. "All right," he whined.

Gran winked at Quinton as she set a stack of pancakes on his plate. "Sounds familiar, huh?"

"Does it?" He feigned ignorance as he doused his pancakes with the warm strawberry syrup that had been left in the middle of the table.

"Mm hmm. I remember a young boy not too long ago, eager to find the perfect tree. He'd scarf down his pancakes, jibber jabbing the entire time. It's a wonder I didn't have pieces of pancakes flying on my food."

Q's face warmed. He didn't recall being that exuberant, but he got the point. "Got it, Gran."

"You do." She paused, measuring him. "I don't say this enough, but I'm right proud of you Quinton Hendricks."

Q nodded at his grandmother, battling back the funny beat in his chest.

"Me too, Gran?" Deuce asked, looking up from his food.

"Sure am Quinton Hendricks, Junior."

Deuce beamed, his baby teeth gleaming with bits of pancakes stuck to them.

Q laughed. "We're going to have fun today. Isn't that right, Deuce?"

"Yes! We're going to get a tree. Drink some hot cocoa." He paused and tilted his head to the side. "Daddy, can we invite my friend?"

"Who?" His eyebrows hiked up. That was the one thing he always felt bad about. Deuce didn't have friends outside their four walls.

"Ms. Kendall, duh."

"Oh." His pulse pounded. Wasn't it too early to do

something with Kendall and his son? His eye twitched. "Buddy, she's working. It's Saturday."

Deuce frowned and his bottom lip poked out. "Are you sure, Daddy?"

Hadn't she mentioned opening today? Granted, she'd been closed Friday, but he'd assumed that was so she could decorate.

"Why don't you call and ask?" Gran looked at him pointedly.

"O-kay." He drew his cell phone out of his back pocket and searched for Kendall in his contacts. Gran and Deuce watched him like a hawk while he waited for Kendall to answer or her voicemail to pick up.

"Hey, Q."

"Hey, Kendall." He swiveled in his seat, facing the hallway instead of the burning curiosity of his grandmother and son. "Is The Cozy Shelf opened today?"

"No, sir. We open Monday. Why? Do you need a book?" A chuckle warmed her voice.

"Actually, I was wondering if you'd like to join me and Deuce today. We're going tree hunting."

"You're going to chop down your own tree?" Something like wonder coated her tone.

"We are."

"I'd love to come. I've never done that before."

"Great. Pick you up in thirty minutes?"

"I'll be ready."

He hit end and looked at Deuce. "Your friend is coming."

"Yes!" He threw a fist pump in the air.

~

Kendall grinned. This place was magnificent. "Rockin' Around the Christmas Tree" blared from nearby speakers at the entrance to the farm. Tree farm employees dressed like elves handed out maps for the farm. Apparently, they had a self-cut and pre-cut area, along with hay rides, sledding area, and snacks and drinks concessions.

She rubbed her gloved hands in anticipation.

"Look, Ms. Kendall." Deuce pointed to a wooden reindeer.

It had a hole cut out to allow people to take a reindeer picture. A line of kids had already started.

"That looks fun."

"Can you take my picture, Daddy?" Deuce looked up, head tilted to take in Q's frame.

"Sure. How about we stand in line?"

"I can grab us some drinks?" Kendall offered.

"That sounds great. We'll take hot chocolates." He pulled out his wallet.

She waved it away. "I got it, Q."

"You sure?" He appeared pensive.

"I'm sure."

"Daddy, come on." Deuce tugged at Q's jacket.

"Thanks, Kendall."

She pivoted on her heel and walked toward the hot chocolate stand. The weather had dipped into the thirties but still no signs of snow. Did that mean they'd get pummeled when it finally came down? She sighed. As much as she loved a white Christmas, she had no desire to be buried in snow with no end in sight.

Think happy thoughts.

She stepped into line just as another lady approached from the side. "I'm sorry." Kendall gestured in front of her. "Go ahead."

"Oh no, that's okay. You have a husband and son waiting for you."

Kendall blinked and slowly turned to glance at Q and Deuce. This woman thought they were a family? Her cheeks heated at the thought and a small fissure of pleasure warmed her heart. "Oh, I don't think they'd mind waiting." Never mind the fact they weren't hers.

"Thank you so much." The woman smiled, showing a little lipstick on her teeth. "I hope you enjoy the day with your men."

Her breath caught. What did she say? Should she correct the woman or let her mind create a fantasy where she belonged to Quinton and he belonged to her? Kendall looked back once more, watching as Q took a picture of Deuce.

Lord, what would it be like to be a true family? One that created traditions of cutting down Christmas trees, drinking hot chocolate in the crisp winter air, with love keeping them together? She sniffed, focusing her eyes on the vendor's menu. They had three sizes of hot chocolate and offered marshmallows, peppermints, and other condiments to go in them.

Yet, her mind had stayed focused on the picturesque scene Q and Deuce created. An ache rent her heart and longing pierced her soul. She'd never had family moments like this before. At least not anything that felt permanent. She'd been fully aware that her mom would leave at any moment's notice. If she were off for a holiday it would be the day itself and not an actual vacation. The longest she'd seen her mom in one setting was for two weeks. And that's because her mom took her to Europe for her high school graduation gift.

Being here with Q and his son made her realize just how lonely most of her life had been. There were no visits to tree farms. Her grandmother had always had a fake tree. Even The Cozy Shelf had a fake tree. When it needed replacing, Kendall did so without a second thought. She had been living life a certain way for so long. Had she inadvertently missed out on something greater?

Her contemplative mood carried with her as she met back up with Quinton.

"Thank you, Ms. Kendall." Deuce carefully held onto his kids' cup of hot chocolate.

"You're welcome." She looked at Q. "I asked them to put half cold water, so it wouldn't burn him."

His mouth dropped open. "Wow. Thank you. I appreciate that." He squatted down. "Deuce, Ms. Kendall asked them to make sure it's not too hot. Can I taste to check?"

"Okay."

Quinton took a sip. "It's perfect."

"I don't have to wait?" Deuce's brown eyes widened.

"No. Drink up."

"Yes," he whispered.

Kendall laughed. "He's adorable."

"Thanks." He nudged her softly with his elbow. "And thanks for thinking of the drink temperature."

"Sure. I've seen Daisy do it with Bliss tons of times."

"How did you two become friends?"

"Lit class." Q stared at her blankly so she expanded. "We met in our college literature class. That's how I met Emma as well."

They strolled toward the self-cut area. Deuce stopped periodically to drink some hot chocolate and then sprinted ahead only to stop and repeat the process.

"What about your friend, Xavier? How did you two meet?" Emma would throttle Kendall if she didn't dig for information for her.

"He's from the city. I met him through church."

NYC? She hadn't pictured that. Maybe it was all the reading material he purchased, but she thought he came from someplace more low key. "Really?"

"Yep. But he's here to stay."

"Heartfalls is pretty great." She sipped her hot cocoa, relishing the taste of peppermint. "Lots more stuff to do in a slower-paced town than in a city."

"Agreed."

They finished walking and found a nearby trash can to throw their cups away. The smell of pine enveloped Kendall as she walked down rows of Christmas trees.

"What about this one?" Deuce tilted his head back to look at a tall one.

"That one won't fit, buddy."

"Okay." His face scrunched up, and he ran down the row. He stopped abruptly and clapped his gloved hands together. "I found it, Daddy!"

Q picked up the pace, and Kendall stretched her legs to keep up. She stopped short as she took in the beautiful tree. A slight breeze blew in the air and added a layer of chill to Kendall's already frozen body. But at the moment, all she could imagine was the tree decorated and placed in a home.

"Beautiful," she whispered.

"I did good?" Deuce asked.

"You did good, son." Q placed a hand on Deuce's shoulder.

Q pulled out a measuring tape and to determine the width of the tree before checking the height. "Oh yeah, this tree is perfect. Not too big, not too small."

"Hooray!" Deuce giggled with excitement.

Kendall's heart dipped in her chest. She could get really attached to these two quickly.

"Let's make sure it's not going to die anytime soon." Quinton reached out and shook the tree.

"What are we looking for?" Kendall asked.

"Lots of dropping pine needles."

"I think I saw a couple."

"Me too."

"Me three!" Deuce chimed.

Quinton circled the tree. "No discoloration. I think it's safe to chop it down."

Kendall bit the inside of her lip, excitement thrumming through her veins. She'd never chopped anything, let alone a tree.

Q squatted to his son's level. "Deuce, you want to saw first?"

Deuce's brown eyes widened, and he nodded his head. Quinton guided his son's hands onto the bow saw.

After a few back-and-forth motions, Deuce backed away. "That's hard work, Daddy. You can do the rest."

Kendall chuckled, her laughter melding with Q's.

"You want a couple of swipes at it, Kendall?"

"Definitely." She sank to her knees and took the bow from Q.

"Just go back and forth. Yep, you've got it."

Kendall beamed at Q and froze. From up close, she

could see the lashes framing his dark brown eyes and smell the hint of chocolate on his breath. Q's eyes shifted as if cataloging her features. Did he find her pretty? Was he as captivated in this moment as she was?

He shifted forward, and her breath caught with anticipation. If he kissed her, she'd melt into a puddle at his feet.

"Are you guys tired?"

Kendall dropped the saw, jumping as Deuce's voice penetrated the hormone-induced fog she'd been in.

"You aren't sawing anymore. Ms. Kendall?"

"No, Deuce." She stood. "I'll let your Daddy handle it from here."

And pray her heart would slow down to just dreaming speed instead of almost kissed.

Chapter Eleven

"You are in every line I have ever read." — Charles Dickens, *Great Expectations*

Q pushed open the door to Tonio's Pizzeria. The smell of cheese and meats wafted in the air, making his mouth water. He glanced around the dining area looking for Xavier. His friend threw an arm in the air, waving him forward. Q walked around tables and booths until he made it to the back wall where Xavier sat.

"Hey, Professor."

Xavier gave a head nod in greeting. "I already ordered."

"The works?"

"You know it."

Q smiled. "Who else is coming?"

"Matt said he'd come and apparently invited Sean."

"Daisy's husband?"

Xavier nodded.

"What do you know about him?"

"Not much. He's good friends with Matt so..."

Quinton sat back in his seat. "He gives off a weird vibe. Do you know what I mean?"

"Seems kind of standoffish but maybe he's an introvert."

"True." Q held out his hands in a what-do-I-know fashion.

"Heads up." Xavier nodded. "They're here."

Q turned around in his seat and waved at the two men heading their way. Normally he'd want his back to the wall, but whenever he ate with Xavier that honor belonged to his friend. Xavier had a real phobia about having his back exposed.

He stood and shook Matt's hand, clapping his back. Then he shook Sean's hand. Q had seen him around Heartfalls, but they didn't really run in the same circles. Come to think of it, he'd never even seen him at church. Although Daisy attended.

"I ordered The Works and some breadsticks," Xavier said.

Matt sat next to Xavier and Sean sat next to him. He shifted his chair over to the right, allowing for more space between them.

Xavier steepled his fingers, resting his chin on them. "The reason I asked you guys to come is twofold."

"How so?" Matt asked.

"Well, first, I wanted to hang out. Get out of the house and go somewhere other than church and work."

"Agreed," Sean uttered.

"Second, I wanted some men to walk alongside me in life. Sort of like accountability partners but with more emphasis on friendship than just keeping us on the straight and narrow."

"I can get behind that." Q looked around the table. "Women get together all the time, but men not so much."

"That's because the world would think it's weird," Sean added.

"But we are not of this world," Matt replied softly. "I think that is why so many men flounder. Have you ever noticed the lack of groups and programs for men at church? I admit Pastor Eli does his best, but it's not the same as for the women."

"But don't they need the connection more than we do?" Sean asked. He straightened. "We're loners."

"But God didn't make us to be that way." Q cleared his throat as all eyes turned to him. "God built us for community. To be the body of Christ. We can't function appropriately if we're all trying to do our own things and leave the connection out of it."

Sean's jaw tightened, and he looked down at his plate.

Not for the first time, Quinton wondered what his story was. He turned to Xavier. "I'm in. Whatever you want this to be." He gestured around the table. "I'm in. Bible study, a group of friends to hang out with, whatever."

"Thanks, man." Xavier nodded at him.

"I'm in as well." Matt gave a sheepish grin. "Most people don't want to invite me to their gatherings. They hear the word pastor and think I'm going to condemn their every action."

Sean chuckled. "They must not know you."

Q stared in amazement. So the guy did have a friendly bone in his body.

"People don't want to get to know someone they think will judge them."

True. And maybe that's why Q and Sean had never clicked. He'd been judging the man from the moment he first laid eyes on him.

"Sounds like we all need to be a part of this then." Q looked at the table.

"Should we label this?" Matt asked. "Are we a Bible study? Club?"

"Don't turn us into girls, Matty boy," Sean remarked. "No labels. Just four guys hanging out."

"Sounds good to me," Q chimed. He had to agree with Sean. Adding a label added a woman's touch that wasn't necessary in this environment.

"Great." Xavier clapped his hands together. "Looks like our food is coming. I'll say grace once the server leaves."

"Two orders of The Works and an order of breadsticks." The server smiled, her ponytail swinging with her movements.

"Thank you," they chorused.

"My pleasure."

Xavier waited a beat before speaking. "Let's pray. Father, we thank You for giving us a heart for fellowship. May we glorify You in all we do, and may You move in our lives. In Jesus' name, Amen."

"Amen." Q grabbed a slice of pizza, inhaling the aroma of the meats mixed in with the veggies. He picked off an olive, savoring the bite. "I love their pizza."

"Mm hmm." Xavier nodded, mouth full of his first bite.

Quinton folded the pizza in half and took a bite. An explosion of cheese, tomato sauce, and herbs greeted him quickly followed by pepperoni and salami.

Silence descended as they filled their stomachs. Reaching for a breadstick, Matt broke the silence first. "How's Bliss, Sean?"

Sean wiped his mouth with the back of his hand. "Good. Nothing came of the incident."

Xavier looked as confused as Q felt. "What happened?" he asked.

"She smashed her finger and because she has sickle cell, it was a concern. We didn't know if it would lead to a pain crisis."

"I'm sorry." Q stared down at his plate. What did you say about something like that?

"We're used to it. It's our normal."

"I'm glad she's okay."

Sean looked at him. "Thank you."

"What's up with you, Q?" Matt asked.

"Yeah. How are the notes coming?" Xavier asked.

"Notes?" Sean looked at him.

Xavier laughed at his look of discomfort and launched into an explanation of the note exchange between him and Kendall.

"Pretty ingenious," Matt said. He took a bite of his breadstick, quickly chewing. "I may have to use a dating website to find a spouse."

"Why? I thought women liked being married to pastors," Q said.

Matt snorted. "You watch too much TV if you believe that."

"It's true." Sean sat back in his chair. "Women have avoided him like the plague since he graduated from seminary."

"So you guys grew up together?" Xavier asked.

They both nodded.

"What about you two?" Sean asked.

"Q is my mentor of sorts. He's helped me through a rough time in my life." Xavier gave him a grateful look.

"And you'd return the favor."

Xavier still had trouble believing he was redeemed. Q could only hope he learned sooner rather than later. There was no sense walking around with an albatross around your neck when Jesus had paid the ultimate sacrifice. Q looked at the men and a prayer formed within his heart.

Lord, may we all help each other remember Your goodness and let go of the things we cannot fix.

Emma propped her feet on Kendall's coffee table, holding a pint of ice cream. "So, you're telling me your first official date included elves and a five-year-old chaperone?" She licked the spoon.

"I don't know if you could consider it a date." Kendall dug into her hazelnut gelati from the local ice cream store.

"I wouldn't. His son was there. You need to quit this meek and quiet game you have going. Just lay it all out there. You like him and want to get to know him. Bam. End of discussion."

"Good grief." She frowned at Emma. "You're starting to sound like Daisy."

Emma curled her lip and then took another lick of ice cream.

"Why don't you just buy cones?"

"It's more fun licking it off a spoon. Plus, I don't have to worry about any ice cream melting and dripping down my hand."

"It's twenty degrees outside. That stuff isn't melting any time soon." She arched an eyebrow. "Besides, we're inside."

"And it's like a furnace in here." Emma wiggled her eyebrows. "You should try it."

"I would feel ridiculous."

"Says the one grinning over hand holding on a bow saw."

"It was romantic."

"And you had gloves on."

Kendall picked up her *I Read Past My Bedtime* pillow and threw it at Emma, who laughed and ducked.

A knock sounded at the window that linked to the fire escape. Kendall turned and then looked at Emma. "Are you expecting anyone?"

"This is your house, you ninny."

Kendall chuckled as she headed for the fire escape. She peeked through the curtains. *Uh oh.* Daisy didn't look too happy, and judging from the person standing next to her, Kendall could guess why. She unlocked the window and pushed it open. "Hey, girl."

"Hey, Kendall," Daisy wrapped her in a hug after coming in. "Help me," she whispered, before pulling back. "This is Paula," she gestured. "Paula, this is my best friend, Kendall."

"Nice to meet you." She motioned toward the living area. "Emma's here."

"Oh." Daisy introduced Emma and Paula.

Kendall stared at Daisy's half-sister. Paula didn't look

like anything she'd expected. She'd assumed that Daisy's half-sister would either be white or Black. But she looked like an Afro-Latina. Her brown skin had a red tint to it and seemed to glow. Her long, black hair hung straight down her back.

"What are you up to?" Daisy asked, sitting in Kendall's vacated spot.

"Gelati," Kendall held up her container.

"Yum," Paula said. "What flavor?"

"Hazelnut."

"They have some amazing flavors in the city." Paula sat next to Daisy. "I miss it."

No one seemed to care that Kendall's couch had been taken over, so she moved across the room to sit with Emma.

"I've been to the city a few times," Emma said. "Too crowded for me."

"Hear, hear," Kendall said before diving back into her ice cream/Italian ice mix.

"It's okay." Daisy looked put out that she had to agree with Paula.

Kendall kept her shoulders still as she tried to suppress her laughter. "How long are you in town for, Paula?"

"Not sure. I needed a change of pace."

That was vague. Daisy was probably climbing the walls.

"What do you do?" Emma asked. She finally stopped licking her spoon. Probably because Daisy was here. Kendall really wished they could get along.

"I was a personal shopper in the city. I'm taking a little hiatus and reevaluating my priorities."

"A personal shopper?" Emma sat up and leaned forward.

Kendall snickered. Emma loved all things clothes and accessories. It was probably the real reason she didn't like the city, not enough closet space.

"Yes, but I doubt I can do that in Heartfalls."

"Then you're thinking of staying here?" Daisy turned to her sister.

Kendall couldn't quite read the look. Despair? Dismay?

"I'm going to look at places to rent tomorrow."

"Oh." Daisy met Kendall's gaze and a sheen of tears covered them.

Kendall bit her lip. She needed to change the subject before Daisy malfunctioned in front of all of them. "I got to help chop down a tree yesterday."

"What?" Paula and Daisy wore twin looks of confusion.

"Q, Deuce, and I went to find a Christmas tree for their house. Q let me take a few sawing motions of the tree."

"Did you decorate it too?" Daisy's eyes had that uncanny bulldozing gleam in her eye.

Any moment she'd probably advise Kendall to marry the man and live happily ever after. Not that it was a bad idea. "I did." She shifted in her seat, uncomfortable with all the attention. "Then Deuce asked me to read a bedtime story."

She had worried that Q would feel replaced; but instead they took turns, each one doing a different voice for the characters. It had been magical and something she'd never envisioned for herself.

Daisy's eyebrows lifted. "Wow, girl. Maybe you'll have a boyfriend finally by the end of the year."

"I'm comfortable at the pace we're moving."

"Snail's pace?" Daisy asked.

Paula shook her head. "Why are you always pushing people? Leave her be."

Daisy's mouth opened, and then snapped shut. Kendall was pretty sure she heard teeth clanging.

"I think we should go." Daisy stood up and marched to the door. "Are you coming?"

"It was nice to meet you." Paula had a look of chagrin on her face as she got up and followed her sister out.

"What was that?" Emma asked.

"I don't know, but they could probably use a prayer."

"Or two or three."

Chapter Twelve

"There is nothing I would not do for those who are really my friends. I have no notion of loving people by halves, it is not my nature."

—Jane Austen, *Northanger Abbey*

The morning rays glistened off the slate blue color of Cayuga Lake. The foliage had withered away while awaiting the first dusting of snow that would cover them in winter's light. Quinton sat back against his mesh camp chair, soaking it all in. Being in the midst of nature was where he felt closest to the Lord. To hear the sounds, view the majesty of the Creator, and be still in His presence. This is what it was all about.

From the moment he'd dropped Kendall off at the shop, his thoughts had been warring against the feelings she evoked and the memories of the past. It had been with him while hanging with his friends and it remained now.

There was something between them that bordered on magical. If he allowed his thoughts to be silenced, Q knew loving Kendall would come with his next breath. Yet the damage his first marriage had left behind had shut down his heart. He could no longer love with his whole self.

But he wanted to change.

So there he sat under the open skies, begging God for an answer. Not to the situation with Kendall, but to the broken pieces a divorce had left behind. It'd altered him to something unrecognizable. Something he wasn't okay with. He wanted to be who he was without forgetting the lessons his first marriage had taught him.

What do I do with that, Lord?

It was like his truck. The interior was brand new with a vintage feel that would serve the F1 well. But the rusty outside showed its past life and what the truck had been through. If he were to cover it up with a nice coat of paint, would it mean the truck was no longer the same?

He groaned, dropping his head into his hands. *Father, I need you. I want to love with the intensity you made me to feel. But I don't want to be hurt again. I'm not sure I could take that pain.* He stared out onto the water, letting the cry of his heart sink in for a moment.

"There is no fear in love; but perfect love casts out fear, because fear involves torment. But he who fears has not been made perfect in love."

The Scripture awakened his mind and pierced his heart. He drew in a ragged breath. Had he not let God have His perfect work in his life? God's love could right any wrongs and empower Q to love in accordance with His plan. He stared down at his hands, always stained, a reminder of his work.

Q gulped. His heart bore the stain of a broken marriage. But God could truly heal him. Be the stain remover that would give Q a new life. He needed to make a commitment to God and himself that he would love wholly by God's power.

Lord, I want to love Kendall Your way and through Your strength. Left to my own devices, I'll fail and hide and never gather the courage to tell her how I feel. I'll always be waiting for the other shoe to drop and for disappointment to set in. But Lord, I feel like she is worthy to love with my whole self. But I need to know that You've put me back together and made me stronger. Not by my own might but empowered with Yours. Please take this fear from me and the worry of what could be and enjoy what's happening now. In Jesus' name, Amen.

Q took one look at the water. The sun had risen a little higher in the sky, painting it with muted colors. He glanced at his watch. Deuce would be up soon, ready to start the day with an intensity and exuberance that had Q wishing he drank coffee. Instead, he asked God for the love needed to make his little boy's day great. This second Sunday of December, they would walk into Heartfalls Community Church.

Deuce always looked forward to church. Deuce was disappointed there were no cars in the Bible, so he picked the next best thing. His favorite Bible story was of Noah and all the animals. The children's church volunteers were amazing. Admittedly, Q looked forward the most to seeing Kendall. If only to say hi and smile, knowing what he'd committed before the Lord.

He knew God would tell him when to share his feelings and for once, the thought didn't send him into a panic. His morning quiet time had righted his soul. It was time to start the day.

~

Her mouth twisted to the side as she stared at her reflection. *It's not going to work.* Kendall sighed, taking off her third outfit. The first two had looked too revealing for a day in church. Granted, no cleavage had shown, but her scoop necked shirts had been lower than she was comfortable with. Emma claimed her necklines were being stretched in the dryer. Maybe she was right. Time to budget for a dry-cleaning bill and save her necklines.

She shrugged and perused the items in her closet again. The chill in the December air meant no dresses, unless she wore tights or leggings underneath. Her eyes widened. She had wool-lined leggings. Kendall walked to her dresser and opened the bottom drawer. There lay her olive-green leggings. She slid them on and walked back to her closet to grab her heather gray sweater dress. Next, she arranged her plaid green-and-gray scarf to hang down the front.

After lightly applying eye shadow and lip gloss, Kendall shook her natural hair free before sliding on a gray headband to give the wild hair a cohesive look. She smiled. It wasn't bad and now she didn't have to change clothes for a fifth time.

Grabbing her Bible and phone, Kendall headed out. Snow flurries flutter before her eyes as Kendall descended the fire escape and made her way over to her blue hatchback in the back of the Victorian shop. The poor car sat there unused most days unless she was meeting her friends or going shopping. There really was no reason to leave her work-home for any other reason.

When Kendall arrived at church, she scanned the parking lot, looking for a certain rusty truck. Disappointment settled in when her gaze refused to find it. Her breath materialized as she marched quickly up the steps in hopes to avoid freezing. She sighed as the warmth of the interior welcomed her. She needed coffee stat. The hospitality team always had flavored creamers out. She wanted peppermint mocha. She lived for the holidays and all the many specialty items that came with it.

Last month she'd had her fill of pumpkin latte creamers. The first sip had a little sting from the heat, but she didn't mind. Her brain wouldn't fire on all cylinders until she'd downed at least half of the contents of her cup.

Footfalls broke through her reverie, and she turned to see who approached. She almost gulped the hot coffee when Quinton came into view. He had on a navy-blue sweater that hugged his body. A simple gold cross hung from his neck.

"Morning, Kendall."

"Morning," she gulped again. *What do I do, Lord? What do I say?*

Hanging out with him and Deuce was supposed to rid her of awkwardness, not increase it.

He slid his hands into his front pockets. "Would you like to come over after church? My grandmother always cooks a nice meal."

Yes! No. Kendall blinked. "Thank you, I..."

"Kendall," squealed Daisy.

Daisy bypassed Kendall's personal bubble and

wrapped an arm around her. "I knew I'd find you by the coffee." She turned her megawatt smile onto Q. "How are you doing this morning, brother?"

"Good. You?"

"Oh, just peachy." Daisy flashed a row of straight teeth.

But Kendall knew her fangs were lurking under the surface. What she didn't understand was why. Daisy had been pushing her to get with Quinton since she'd laid eyes on him.

"I just need to borrow Kendall for a moment. M'kay?"

"Sure thing. Text me later?"

Kendall nodded, and Q left with a wave.

She turned to Daisy. "What on earth is wrong with you, Daisy?"

"Paula is driving me mad. She went to drop off Bliss at children's church. I just had to get away from her."

"What did she do?"

"What didn't she do?" Daisy sneered. "Talking about all her trips with Dad and her wonderful life in the city. If I have to hear one more thing, I'm going to gag. That should shut her up."

Kendall stared at her friend, her eyes widening with each rant that left Daisy's lips. She'd never seen Daisy so riled up. And she thought their college graduation had been bad. Nothing compared to the words vomiting from Daisy's broken soul right now. She laid a hand on Daisy's shoulders, meeting her gaze.

"Paula is your sister. She's not responsible for what happened between your parents. She's not responsible for how your dad interacts with you. Maybe she's dealing with problems too."

"Like what?" Daisy snorted, folding her arms across her chest.

"You'll never know unless you ask."

Daisy's mouth parted slightly, and a look of confusion passed across her face. "Do you really think something could be wrong?"

"Why else would she run to her big sister?"

Daisy bit her lip. "I'm acting ridiculous, aren't I?"

"I love you, Daisy."

"Ouch." She winced. "That bad, huh?"

"God loves you too." Kendall bit the inside of her lip to keep them from twitching.

"Oh you." Daisy lightly slapped her on the arm. "I get it. I'm a bear and slightly evil."

"Maybe more than slightly." Emma said, walking up to them.

Daisy rolled her eyes, and Kendall's gut clenched. Would they start fighting just after she'd calmed the beast in Daisy?

"Today I may have deserved that."

"Oh, I can keep going." Emma pushed her long hair over her shoulder.

"Please don't, Em." Kendall hugged the side of her friend. "You're better than that," she whispered.

"Save 'em for later," Daisy smirked.

Kendall shook her head. "Let's go find a spot to sit."

"Oh hey," Daisy said as they strolled for the sanctuary's double doors. "What did Q want?"

"You were talking to Q?" Emma squeezed her hand.

"He invited me to lunch at his house."

Daisy's mouth dropped, and Emma gasped. "What did you say?"

"I didn't have time to respond. Daisy had a crisis."

"Oh, no." Daisy slapped her forehead. "I'm so self-absorbed and sorry, Kendall."

She shrugged. She hadn't known what to say anyway. "It's okay."

"You're going, right?" Emma and Daisy asked simultaneously.

"I guess that's my answer."

They entered the sanctuary and a hush fell over them. The hairs on her arms stood as the shimmering sound of the drum's cymbals built anticipation. Quietly, the three slid into a row. Kendall placed her Bible and phone on the chair's arm rest. She put her phone on silent and then turned to the front as the worship leader sang the first notes.

Chills went up her spine as the lyrics to "Revelation Song" opened the air. Ann had a voice just as sweet and angelic sounding as the recording artist, Kari Jobe. Every time she sung, Kendall could imagine the angels joining in and worshipping the Lord in the throne room. She bowed her head, lifting arms to the sky as the words flowed over her.

Kendall let all of her cares float away as she joined in singing the chorus. Today wasn't about her. It wasn't even about Quinton and the feelings that swirled around her whenever he was near. Today was about the Creator of the universe who cared enough about her to know the number of hairs on her head. Considering she had a lot, she had a hint of the depth of His love for her.

She smiled, reveling in the presence of God and the promise of His love.

Unfortunately, the rightness didn't remain. Her

thoughts brought Q back to mind. Was she going too fast? Was she letting her feelings rule her and drag her into a relationship that should be savored in the moments instead of rushed to the altar?

Lord, please guide me. Don't let my emotions get the better of me. I don't want to be a slave to them. I don't want to choose the wrong guy because of a few butterflies. Granted it was more like heart palpations when Q was around. Like her heart forgot to beat lub-dub and beat Quin-ton instead.

She rolled her eyes at the cheesy-factor of her thoughts. *See, Lord, this is what I mean. I romanticize every single thing about a guy. I want what You want for my life. I want Your will to reign and my emotions and feelings to take a back seat.*

Kendall shook her head. *No, that's not right. I want to be able to trust my feelings for Q. To know He's what You have for me and that he's not just some crush.* Because she was too old for that now. Not that having a crush was wrong, but letting it rule her every waking moment...yeah, she was *so* over that.

Chapter Thirteen

"Till I loved I never lived." — Emily Dickinson

This.

This was what life was all about. Family, food, and love binding them together. Quinton glanced at Kendall out of the side of his eyes. Okay so love may not yet bind them, at least on her end, but he'd seen a hint of promise in her eyes. When he'd received the YES message on his cell, pure pleasure had raced through him.

Before he'd had his talk with God, Q would have agonized over her lack of immediate response. He would have come up with a list of rejections she was probably formulating in her mind. Now, he saw things differently. What he saw as rejection now appeared to be good old-fashion caution. And *that* he could appreciate.

Kendall would remain a fixture in his life just for owning The Cozy Shelf. He didn't see her as a flight risk.

And he knew now if they didn't work out, that neither he nor Deuce would be crushed. But he had a good feeling it wouldn't come to that. God was working on his heart and he had to believe Kendall's as well.

"Daddy, can I dip my biscuit in the stew?" Deuce's big brown eyes held a hopeful sheen to them.

"Sure, buddy. Just do it slowly and don't stuff the whole thing in your mouth."

Kendall's shoulders shook as she tilted her head toward him. "Will he really put the whole thing in his mouth?" She murmured.

"Unfortunately," he whispered back. He was glad Gran had insisted Kendall sit next to him as she and his father took the ends of the table. Deuce sat across from them.

"Ms. Kendall, how's business at The Cozy Shelf?" Q's dad looked Kendall squarely in the eye.

"It's good. Sales went down from second to third quarter, but with Christmas coming around sales have been on an uptick."

His dad nodded. "Same at the shop. Everyone wants to get repairs done, so they can head out of town for the holidays."

"I would have thought they'd go down so close to Christmas."

"Can't avoid tires and oil changes if you're driving."

"True." She took a bite of her stew.

"Your grandmother would be so proud of you." Gran's wizened face lifted, some wrinkles trying to drag her smile back down.

"Thank you so much. I miss her." Kendall looked down into her bowl.

"I can imagine so. Haven't seen much of your mama."

"She's still flying."

"No chance of retiring?" Q's dad asked.

"Not in the near future. She did mention she was coming for Christmas."

Just then, Q realized they'd never talked about their families. What did he know about the woman beside him? More importantly, how could he get to know everything about her? What made her tick? What made her melt with affection?

He grabbed his water, the need to cool himself rising within him.

"You two are more than welcome to join us for Christmas." His gran offered. "It'll be just us four."

Q turned to Kendall. What did she think of the offer? She raised her head and met his gaze. "I'd like that," she said softly.

"So would I," he murmured.

Man, he wanted to kiss her. Instead he piled his spoon high with stew and filled his mouth. If he couldn't lean over and kiss her, he needed to occupy his thoughts with something else. Like the mouthwatering stew his gran made.

"Kendall," his dad started. "Wednesday, we're going up to the lake for the Fire Carols display. Would you like to join us?"

Q's thoughts had been so consumed of all things Kendall he'd almost forgotten the awesome fireworks display that lit the night sky to Christmas music.

"Oh, I love watching it. I haven't been able to go the past two years, so that would be extra special."

His father smiled. "Great. We'll leave around five, or is your store still open then?"

"No, it closes at five p.m. It might take me about ten to fifteen minutes to get over here."

"I'll come get you," Q spoke up. "That way we can just head there from the store."

"Thanks, Q."

"Perfect." His dad scooted back, his chair scraping against the floor. "If you don't mind, I need a nap. A perfect way to celebrate this Sunday." He turned to look at Kendall. "It was a pleasure."

"Likewise."

"Naps are awful, Grandpa," Deuce said around a mouthful of biscuit.

"Not at my age, my boy."

"I'm going to go ahead and leave as well." His gran rose slowly, hands flat on the table top for leverage.

"You need help, Gran?" He half rose, halting as she waved a hand at him.

"I've got it. These old bones just needed a moment." She turned toward Kendall. "Nice to see you again, Kendall."

"Likewise, Mrs. Hendricks."

His gran waved and shuffled out of the room.

Kendall rested her chin in the palm of her hand, staring at Deuce. "Is that biscuit good, Deuce?"

"Mm hmm." His eyes widened. "Want some?" He held out the remnants of his biscuit, dripping with stew gravy.

"No, thank you. I have my own." She held up a biscuit, and then dunked it into her food. Taking a bite, her cheeks bunched up and her eyes lit with pleasure.

"Good, huh?" Pieces of food flew from Deuce's mouth.

"No talking with food in your mouth, buddy."

"Sorry, Daddy." He dipped his head, sneaking pieces of his biscuit into his mouth.

"It's all right. Try and remember."

"'Kay." He stared down at his placemat and frowned. "Can I have another biscuit?"

"Why don't you eat the carrots?"

His nose wrinkled, and he shook his head fast.

"But carrots are good." Kendall made a show of filling her spoon with the vegetables and taking a huge bite. "Yum," she mumbled.

Deuce's mouth dropped open as Kendall took another bite. Q loaded his spoon up and followed.

"You too?" Deuce asked, looking at Q.

"They make you strong, Deuce." Kendall said.

"Daddy strong?"

Kendall examined him, and his heart stopped. Then speeded up, thumping with pleasure at the look in her eyes. "Just like your dad."

"Okay." He took a bite and began chewing. His nose scrunched up and his eyes began to water but Deuce continued to chew until he swallowed the last pieces. "Ugh. Can I have something to drink?"

"Sure." Q pointed to the counter. "There's some milk over there."

Deuce grabbed the small plastic cup that was half full of milk.

"Contrary to belief, Deuce *will* be taking a nap." Q stated.

"Aw, Dad."

He swiveled in his chair to face Kendall. "Would you like to watch a movie while he naps?"

Mischief lit her eyes. "I believe it's your pick."

"You'd be right." He winked at her, taking pleasure in the pinkening of her cheeks. "I'll be back."

She nodded.

"Come on, Deuce. Nap time."

His son poked his bottom lip out. "Bye, Ms. Kendall."

"Enjoy that nap and dream of wardrobes for me, Deuce."

"Yes, ma'am!"

~

Kendall tucked her feet under her as she cozied into the corner of the love seat. Q stood up from the DVD player and headed straight for her. She swallowed as she took in his presence. The prayer to seek God's pacing had completely gone out the window the moment she sat next to him at dinner. And when he'd winked at her—goodness, she'd felt the need for CPR after that.

He sat down, the couch dipping under his weight, and spread his arms along the sofa back. "I picked an old favorite."

"An action film?"

"Kind of. You'll see."

She turned her attention to the movie all the while aware of every move he made. As a trailer came on, Kendall faced Q. "Can I ask you a question?"

"Sure."

"What happened to Deuce's mom?" She held her breath. Would he be upset? Tell her she had no right to know?

"She left when he was a couple of months old. Didn't want to be married or be a mom."

Pain rose in her throat, and Kendall pressed a hand upon her heart. "Has she seen him since?"

Q shook his head wordlessly.

"Oh, Q."

"We're okay." His eyes filled with certainty. "It was tough, but my dad and gran helped out a lot."

"But the hurt you must have gone through..." Her voice trailed off as she fought the tears that wanted to rise.

Q cupped her cheek. "I'm okay. Life is looking up for me. I met this amazing woman who owns a bookstore."

Her lips quirked to the side. "What if..."

"You're worth any potential heartache."

She leaned into his hands as the ache in her chest for Q's loss changed to an ache of longing. "You don't know much about me."

He slid his hand down her cheek and gripped her hand. "But I will. There's no rush, Kendall."

Tears filled her eyes. How had he known? His honesty deserved the same from her. "I was married before."

"Really?" He moved back as if to take her in more fully. "What happened?"

She wanted to pull her hands away. To create distance before bearing her soul in front of this man who had taken up residence in her heart way too fast for her comfort.

"He found someone better." She licked her lips. "We didn't really have anything in common. At least nothing that would keep him around."

"What about love?"

Her eyes smarted. "Apparently not," she croaked out.

"His loss."

Kendall's head snapped up. Q peered down at her with a softness, and something else she couldn't quite place.

Q motioned to the TV. "You ready to start?"

She nodded, and then turned back to face it. *Confessional now closed.* She smirked at the thought but was glad that it pushed the sadness back a bit. "Get Smart?" Her brows wrinkled in confusion as the title of the movie filled the screen.

"Have you seen it?"

"No."

"You'll love it. Just the movie we need to keep you from bawling into your coffee cup."

"Hey!"

He chuckled and pressed play on the remote. "Okay, fine. Keep us both from crying?"

"That sounds better."

"No crying movies here, Ms. Jackson."

"I'm okay with that."

"Good. Now hush and watch the movie." He winked.

Her lips curved involuntarily. As she watched the opening scene, a brush of fingers caught her attention. She looked down and saw Q's hand laying palm upward. *Courage.* She placed her hand in his and sighed as he laced their fingers together.

Everything was going to be okay.

Chapter Fourteen

"In vain have I struggled. It will not do. My feelings will not be repressed. You must allow me to tell you how ardently I admire and love you."

—Jane Austen, *Pride and Prejudice*

A strong urge to get to Kendall's store had woken Q bright and early. It wasn't like he had to do any shopping. He completed all his shopping with ten days to spare. He tapped the steering wheel, trying to figure out what to do. The auto shop didn't open until nine, so he didn't have to be there in a hurry. The Cozy Shelf opened at eight, probably for all the coffee addicts who didn't want to pay high prices at the chain places. But his watch told him it was only seven. Just because he was wide awake didn't mean anyone else was.

"I'm going."

He put the truck in drive and headed for Kendall's store. If she wasn't up, surely she wouldn't hear a knock at the door. Of course, he could text her and see if she was up. But if she wasn't, would it wake her?

Q blinked, realizing snow had started to fall. Not the light flurries that had teased him here and there, but a nice steady fall. He parked and got out to gaze above. The sky was covered with clouds, but nothing angry or ominous looking. Hopefully they would only receive a couple of inches. He'd forgotten to check the weather after reflecting on today's Bible verse.

With a tug on his zipper, he closed his jacket, preventing the wind chill from getting to him. Thankfully, his knit cap helped keep his body warm. He knocked on the door and quietly waited. If Kendall was upstairs she'd never hear him, but maybe it would be a sign. If she was here, he could tell her what had been pressing on his heart from the moment his eyes flicked open.

He raised his hand to knock again and stopped as the door opened.

"Q?"

"Morning."

"Good morning." A soft smile graced her pink lips. "What are you doing here?" She shook her head. "Come on in. I didn't realize it was snowing."

He chuckled. "I had the same thought when I saw it falling onto the car."

"Something on your mind?" She tied her gray sweater close, covering the words written on her shirt.

Not before he read the words *Books, books, and books.*

"Q?"

"Oh, yes." He cleared his throat, clasping his hands together. "I just wanted to talk to you for a moment."

Kendall glanced at the wall clock. "All right. Would you like to come up for a moment? Maybe have some water?" Her eyes lit with mirth.

"That sounds good but no need for the water." He gave her an answering grin.

"Come on."

Kendall led the way, and with each step, the nerves compounded. His palms felt clammy, his heart seemed to beat in his throat instead of his chest. And his stomach… good thing he'd skipped breakfast this morning.

The object of his affection opened her front door and headed straight for her couch. She sat down and motioned for him to do the same. "No, thanks. I think I should stand." Or he'd lose all nerve at baring his heart.

"Okay." She slid her hands between her knees. "Is everything okay?"

He nodded, his tongue becoming tied up.

"Whatever it is, just tell me, Q."

"I love you."

Her eyes widened, and she straightened.

"I love you. I've been terrified of loving you because my ex-wife shattered my heart. I didn't want to come to you with only pieces remaining and say, hey be with me. I also was terrified that you'd reject me." He gasped for air, rubbing a clammy palm down his thigh. "But I can't keep it a secret anymore. God's calling me to love fully and completely. I can't do it in halves, Kendall. I can't even do it with the promise that you'll love me back. And I know there's a chance you're freaking out inside, but I just had to let you know how much I love you."

He sank to the couch and cupped her face. "I love everything about you. The things I know, the things I haven't yet discovered. The way you make my heart race. The way my lips ached to join yours. Most of all, I love the courage it took to slip me those notes and share your heart with me."

"Quinton," she whispered. She closed her eyes and pulled away from his touch.

His heart stuttered at the loss. Was he wrong? Did he come on too strong?

Kendall pushed away from the couch. She wrapped her hands around her middle, staring into his eyes. Where he'd hoped to see joy, he saw nothing but anguish.

"I can't imagine what it took to say all of that." She visibly swallowed.

"But..."

"But I'm just not ready to say those words."

He stood, sliding his hands into his pockets. "And that's understandable. I'm not asking for you to say it back. I'm telling you I can't hide it from you any longer."

"Feelings are fickle, Q."

Agreed. Why had she turned cold on him? "What are you afraid of, Kendall?"

Her eyes filled with tears. "Too many things to count."

"Share one."

She shook her head, bowing it. "I can't," she gasped.

His arms ached to wrap her in a hug. Obviously she struggled with some kind of problem. Some internal hurt she wasn't strong enough to voice.

Be strong.

Q swallowed around the lump in his throat. "I love you

now and forever, Kendall. That's not going to change. It won't go away. *I* won't go away."

A hiccupped sob reached his ears. *Oh, forget boundaries.* He took the two steps necessary to wrap her in his arms and settled her against his chest. She clung to him as her shoulders shook with her silent cries.

Finally she pulled away, wiping at tears streaming down her face. "Could you please leave?"

"Kendall..."

"Please, Q."

His Adam's apple bobbed. "I'll leave for now, but I promise you I *will* come back."

He wasn't sure how he managed to make it to the first floor without tripping over his feet. All the reactions he'd imagined, crying buckets and throwing him out wasn't one of them. Q stopped and glanced over his shoulder. He wanted to go back up there and tell her it would be okay. That he'd wait forever if need be, but the part that had been hurt in the past wanted to hide and maybe even shed a tear or two.

Q shuffled to the front door of The Cozy Shelf and halted. It was a whiteout. The road was no longer visible beneath the blanket of snow that covered it. Even his rust colored truck looked more festive veiled in snow.

"Why, Lord?" He whispered.

Judging by the snow piled around his truck, he wouldn't be driving off into the sunset anytime soon.

~

Kendall stared at the door, tears streaming down her face. What had just happened? Never in a million years had she imagined Q sweeping into her home to declare his love for her. Her heart had shattered into a million pieces.

And she had no idea why.

What is wrong with me?

She had been given another chance at love and it terrified her. From the top of her hair to the tingling in her toes, she felt wrecked and numb all at once.

Kendall flopped down onto her seat and dropped her head into her hands. *Lord, what did I just do? Didn't I ask for courage? But all I feel is an overwhelming sense of fear. This is too fast, Lord. It's too similar to my relationship with Ty. I want to be loved, but I don't want to lose myself.*

"Love suffers long and is kind...love never fails."

And wasn't that the crux of it? She didn't want to suffer. Had suffered enough already.

"Love never fails."

But hadn't it? Ty had left her without a backward glance. He'd found someone more interesting and forsook their vows. Left her in the cold, alone to pick up the pieces of her life. But if she were honest with herself, it wasn't a broken heart but wounded vanity that had left a scar.

Would she ever be enough for someone to stick around? If her own mother couldn't be bothered to stick by her, how could she expect anyone else to want to be around her? Maybe it's why she'd chosen poorly in Ty. Or maybe there was something wrong with her and why he left without a second thought.

"I love you, Kendall. That's not going to change. It won't go away. I won't go away."

"But you kicked him out," Kendall whispered.

She couldn't hold Q to his promise. Not after telling him to leave. A knock sounded, shaking her from her musings. A gasp tore from her lips as she rose. Her knees knocked from the emotions swirling in her midsection. Only one person could be knocking on her door.

Leave.

Had Quinton come back?

I promise you I'll come back.

She opened the door and stared in bewilderment. "Q?"

"Looks like there's a blizzard." His brow furrowed.

So he hadn't come back for her. Her heart dropped to her toes as she stepped back to let him in.

"Look," Q rubbed a hand across the top of his head. "I know you need space. I know I was supposed to leave and let you work everything out. I'm not trying to disrespect that. I had every intention of leaving, but my truck is already buried. I can hang out downstairs in the store, so you can still process." He stopped and met her gaze, his dark eyes probing. "But please, Kendall, don't shut me out. Don't let your mind lead you to some conclusion that is completely false because you won't talk to me."

He came back.

Yes, a snow storm had forced his hand, but he *came back*. Her feet picked up speed, propelling her forward, and Kendall threw her arms around Q's neck.

"Umph." Muffled against her hair as Q wrapped his arms around her, squeezing her tight.

His chin rested on her head as she tucked herself

beneath it, relishing the feel of his arms around her. "I'm sorry."

"Nothing to be sorry for." His arms tightened, remaining firm and secure around her.

"I'm scared."

"Perfect love casts out fear. It's something the Spirit reminded me of this morning."

She pulled away to peer up at him. "Isn't that pertaining to God?"

"Isn't He the one that gives us the power to love others?"

Huh. "Yes."

He smoothed a hand down her cheek. "Then know it will be okay." He took her hand in his and led them to her sofa. "I'm not asking for your hand in marriage. I'm just asking that you give us a chance to get to that point of happily ever after." He gestured toward the stack of books on her coffee table. "Maybe a happily ever after that rivals those."

I want that, Lord. It was like God saw her fears and answered them with quiet acceptance in Quinton's actions.

"That would be amazing." She stared at Q, cataloging his features. "I have a question."

"Anything." He laid his other hand on top of hers.

"Did you leave those notes?"

His lips widened in a cheek-splitting grin, flashing a small dimple she had never noticed before.

A dimple and a cleft chin? *Swoon.* She was a goner.

"I did. I didn't know how to say how I felt, so a friend suggested I write a note." He sat back, still holding onto her hand. "You may have noticed my words aren't poetic or filled with big words. I'm a simple man who lives a simple life and I knew you deserved more than that."

"Q," she whispered.

"I'd read every romance book you've ever read if it means learning how to tell you how much I feel. You deserve the best of me."

A tear slid down her cheek. "I didn't know what to say either."

"Aren't we a pair?" He leaned forward, lightly touching his forehead to hers.

Chapter Fifteen

"Love looks not with the eyes, but with the mind, And therefore is winged Cupid painted blind." — William Shakespeare, *A Midsummer Night's Dream*

"Have you really read every book on this board?" Q rolled the dice and moved his whale eight paces as he waited for Kendall's answer.

"Of course I have. I was an English major, which despite what most people think, has nothing to do with grammar. My courses were predominantly literature courses. Besides that, some of these I read as a child." She looked where he landed and smiled.

"You owe me. I own *Black Beauty*." She rubbed her hands with glee. "And that's an example of a book I read as a child."

He shook his head, shelling out the money. Q had

never even heard of *Bookopoly* until Kendall had removed the board game from her closet shelf. Her Wi-Fi had lost connection half an hour ago. Since she couldn't access Netflix, they'd opted to pass the time playing board games. When he'd called home to tell them he was snowed in, his dad had assured him Deuce was glued to the TV and not to worry. Thankfully, there were a bunch of DVDs there to keep Deuce occupied.

Q focused on the board game which rested on the coffee table. The game was just like Monopoly but featured famous books and genre categories instead of locations and places. It was pretty clever, and Kendall obviously adored it. She was racking up money left and right. Pretty soon he'd have to declare bankruptcy.

"Why do you like reading so much?"

She cocked her head as she shook the dice in her hand. "My mom wasn't around much. She's a flight attendant and was always off to some exotic place." She licked her lips nervously. "It started with her buying me books from those trips, and then I became enthralled by the worlds each author created. Now, I'm just a book nerd." She grinned with pleasure as she moved her eyeglasses token. "What about you? Why do you read or not?"

"Well I read to Deuce each night. We've been working our way through the ones you or the library recommend. I always figured those who read as kids will be smart, and I want him to be smarter than me."

Kendall's mouth dropped open. "You think you're dumb?"

"Not dumb." Heat flushed up his neck. "But not that smart either."

"Do you know what kind of skill and knowledge it takes to restore a car?" Her voice went up an octave.

He shifted in his seat, uncomfortable under her scrutiny. "Yes. I've done it a time or two."

"So why would you think you're not smart?"

His lips twitched. "I stand corrected."

"Good. As long as you know." She winked and held out a hand. "My money?"

"What?"

She held up a knowledge card. "You owe me $20 for judging a book by its cover."

He groaned at the cliché but slid his money over. "I think I'm going to cry uncle."

"Really?" Her bottom lip poked out.

Odd how much he didn't want to deny her. "Maybe we can play another game?" He glanced at the stack of books resting on the other end of the coffee table.

Don't suggest it.

He looked at the sadness in her eyes. "Or maybe you could read a book to me?"

"For real?" Her head popped up, her burgundy eyes widening with a spark of pleasure.

What had he gotten himself into? "For real."

"Hmm, now what to choose?" She tapped her lip with a finger.

Her very kissable lips. When he had strolled back into her flat and seen her in tears, it had taken all his will power not to kiss them away. But considering they were snowed in, he needed to keep his mind fixed on anything other than the way her pink lips begged to be kissed.

Divert, divert, divert!

Quinton reached over and grabbed the first book. "*Count Me In*?"

"It was a recommendation from the Bookish Fiends."

"Come again?"

She laughed. "You know, Jane, right? Guards the hospitality table at church like a mama eagle?"

"Oh, yeah. She can send a glare so chilling you'll be running for a hot beverage."

"Exactly. She runs the book club, Bookish Fiends. The girls decided to read only Indie authors this year. And now I'm learning about a whole new set of authors."

"And *Count Me In* is an Indie book?" At her nod, he continued. "What does that even mean?"

"Oh, just that the person published the book themselves versus going through a traditional publisher."

"Huh. Is it any good?"

"I haven't started it yet. You interested?"

"Sure."

Kendall grabbed the book and sat down on the sofa. She curled her legs underneath her while he sat on the other cushion. It was a little ridiculous for him to hug the armrest, but the more distance between them, the better.

"Okay. Here goes." She cleared her throat, cracking her neck left and right.

He laughed. Couldn't help it. She looked like she was preparing to workout, not read.

"What?" She looked at him innocently. "I have to get my book reading muscles ready."

"Shouldn't that be your eyes?"

She rolled them. "Of course. I stare at the front door at the end of every chapter, so my eyes get a break from having to focus up close. It's no use though." She grabbed a pair of eyeglasses from the end table. "I still ended up wearing these."

"You look cute."

"Thank you." Her cheeks pinked, and her gaze fell back to the book.

"The little hairs on the back of Allegra Spencer's neck stood at attention."

"Wait a minute. Her name is Allegra?"

"That's what it says."

"Why Allegra?"

Kendall huffed. "I don't know, Q. Should we stalk the author on social media and ask her?"

"What's the author's name again?"

"Mikal Dawn." Her brow furrowed. "It's spelled kind of weird but I'm pretty sure it's pronounced Michael."

"Then maybe that's why she gave her character a weird name."

Kendall shrugged. "Continuing on."

"He was behind her."

"Wait, who?"

"Are you going to interrupt me at every sentence?"

"I'll try not to." He stifled a chuckle at the look of exasperation on her face.

"Thanks. Now, where were we?"

"'He was behind her.'"

"Right."

"He was behind her. She could feel his presence as sure as she could smell the beans being ground by the barista on the other side of the reclaimed-wood counter."

"Another coffee hound, huh?"

"Quinton Hendricks, hush!" Kendall covered a finger over her lips.

Her very kissable lips.

Divert, divert, divert!

~

Q's eyes darkened at her admonishment, yet, it wasn't in consternation. At least, she didn't think so. His eyes were almost...smoldering. Kendall tried to swallow, but her mouth had suddenly become as dry as her skin in the New York winter wind.

Did her hair look a mess? Did the way her t-shirt and jeans accentuate her figure make her look undesirable?

He's leaning forward you fool! Of course you look desirable.

And as eager as she was to kiss him, Kendall was also a nervous wreck. She jumped up from the couch, placing her cold hands to her hot face. "I…I don't think that's a good idea."

Her voice seemed to echo in the quiet, sounding far louder than she'd intended.

A sigh greeted her ears. "You're right. We're stuck in here, and the last thing either one of us needs to deal with is a temptation we can't run from."

She nodded, still refusing to turn around. "Exactly."

"But you look so kissable," Q groaned.

"Don't say that." Her heart pounded, and heat flooded her stomach. It would be easy to just march over to the couch and kiss him until her lips tingled.

Okay, so they were tingling now. She rushed to the kitchen area and poured herself a glass of ice water. Maybe they shouldn't stay in her flat. She could always kick him out. There were plenty of spots to sleep downstairs. Masterpiece Corner and Adventure cove had window seats, complete with pillows and cushions.

She tensed, sensing him behind her.

"Kendall?"

Now she knew what that author, Mikal Dawn meant. How could she *not* know Q was behind her? His ocean scent was back, complete with a dash of motor oil and man. All Quinton Hendricks.

"Do you want me to go downstairs?"

Kendall whirled around. "No, but yes."

A lazy grin curved across his lips. "I completely understand. It's probably for the best."

"Is it?"

His eyes squeezed tight. "Please don't look at me like that. My will power is on shaky ground."

"But it's just a kiss? Isn't it?" She licked her lips, nerves spiking her internal thermostat to desert proportions.

"Is it?" He placed a hand on each side of her, trapping her against the counter. "Would it feel simply like two pairs of lips meeting?" He leaned forward, his mouth inches away from hers.

"Of course," she cleared her throat. "That's what kissing is all about."

"It's more, a lot more. And if you don't know that, you haven't been kissed right."

He inched forward, and the pulse in her neck pounded from his closeness. She could see flecks of black in his brown eyes. How did the color manage to be more spectacular than any shade in a crayon box and just as mesmerizing as any jewel? The stubble gracing his upper lip made her wonder how it would feel against her skin.

Wowzers. We haven't even kissed.

"You could change that," she challenged.

His eyes darkened. "I will."

Q moved achingly slow and Kendall didn't want to miss a single moment. She kept her eyes focused on his until his lips greeted hers, and then they closed with pleasure. A hint of homecoming hit her heart, and she understood what he meant. It was much more than physical interaction.

A hint of mint tantalized her as the pressure of his lips increased. All the while, he kept his hands on the counter, and she tightened hers around the cup. Each move of his lips was achingly slow and sweetly tender. A tear slid down her cheek at the beauty of it.

Q broke the kiss, resting his forehead on hers before pressing a brief kiss to her forehead. He stepped back and paused, surprise crossing his face as he took in the sight of her tear. She wiped it away as her cheeks flushed with embarrassment.

"Hey, no need to be embarrassed." He wiped her face with his thumbs. "I love you."

She gulped.

"I'm going downstairs." He walked backwards. "Will you be okay up here?"

"Yes." She cleared her throat. "Let me get you some blankets and a pillow." She moved to the storage closet.

"Do you have a shovel?"

Kendall paused, raising an eyebrow. "A shovel?"

"Yes. That way you won't be barricaded in."

"Do you think it's wise to go out in a blizzard?"

"Probably not, but I could use a little cooling off."

Her cheeks reddened even more, and she pointed to the wardrobe next to her front door. "In there." She handed him the blankets and pillow. "Come back up at noon and I'll fix you some lunch."

"You don't have to."

"Then you'll waste away before you ever hear me tell you how I feel."

A glint lit his eyes. "Okay then. See you for lunch."

With that, he walked out of her apartment.

Chapter Sixteen

"The course of true love never did run smooth." — William Shakespeare, *A Midsummer Night's Dream*

Quinton blew on his fingers, trying to bring warmth back into them. Shoveling The Cozy Shelf's front porch had been a bear. The snow hadn't let up, but at least he wouldn't have to shovel a mound later on. Thankfully he'd worked up an appetite. He placed the shovel on the mat in front of the door. By the time he finished lunch, he'd need to do another round of shoveling to keep it from icing and becoming a bigger pain once it stopped.

He took the stairs slowly in order to pray.

Father, thank You for bringing Kendall into my life. Lord, I need Your strength right now. I knew kissing her would be powerful, but I didn't expect such a punch. Or her tears. His chest warmed. *Please don't let me give into temptation. Please help us keep it as platonic as possible.*

He shook his head. His feelings were in no way platonic.

Her front door came into view, and he sent another plea heavenward. *Amen.*

Knocking, Q slid his hands into his pockets so he wouldn't be tempted to reach out and touch Kendall.

"How did it go?" Kendall leaned against the door.

"Not bad. I'm sure I'll have to shovel some more after lunch."

"Is it still coming down?" She motioned him inside.

"Like crazy. Anything on the news front?"

"No. My cell isn't getting any reception, and I don't have cable."

Q stopped and looked at her. "I know you like books, but what have you got against TV?"

She laughed. "Nothing. I'm against the cable bill."

"Ah, well, I get that. Deuce would lose his mind if we didn't have any cartoons for him to watch."

"You could always make him play board games." She winked.

"No, ma'am." He shuddered as he draped his jacket on the coat rack. "He gets an insane gleam in his eyes when he plays *Candy Land.*"

"Really?" Kendall's laughter tinkled in the air like glass Christmas ornaments. She placed two bowls on the table, and then turned back to grab a plate of bread.

"Oh yes." He looked into the bowls. *Loaded potato soup. Yum.* Where was he? "Deuce isn't happy unless everyone bows down in defeat. He's the same way with *Chutes and Ladders*, if only a touch more manic."

She covered her mouth, snickering behind her hand as she sank into her dining chair.

He quickly followed suit.

"But Deuce is so sweet. I can't imagine that side of him."

"Come to dinner once the snow leaves. Then see what happens when you mention board games."

"Sounds like fun."

He raised an eyebrow. "Says the crazy lady stealing everyone's money in *Bookopoly*."

"Hey! It's not my fault you don't have good business sense."

He chuckled and motioned to the table. "Should I say grace?"

"Yes, please."

He reached for her hands and bowed his head. "Father, thank You for this meal and the hands that prepared it. May it warm our souls and nourish us. Amen."

"Amen." Kendall smiled at him. "That was beautiful."

And so are you. "Just a simple prayer we say at home."

"Did you live with your dad when you were married?" Kendall spooned some soup into her mouth.

And let's dive right into awkward. "No actually. I moved back shortly after."

"Where were you living?"

He tore a chunk of bread off and dunked it into his soup. "I was stationed in Texas when my ex left us. My service was complete six months later, and that's when we moved back to Heartfalls."

"Wow."

"And you lived in Syracuse before opening the shop, right?"

"No, in Heartfalls."

"What?" He looked up at her. "I don't remember seeing you before the shop opened."

"You've always been preoccupied with Deuce."

He set his spoon down. "Wait a minute. You noticed me?"

"Of course I did." She looked down into her bowl in order to ignore his probing look.

Had he been so caught up in his own misery that he'd missed seeing Kendall around town? What would his life have been like if he'd pursued her sooner?

Past is the past. Leave it there, Q.

Besides, he had been in no shape to enter into another relationship. Deuce had seemed to cry a little too much as a baby. By the time the boy could walk, they'd settled into a routine. Albeit, one that had him running after Deuce and grabbing things within reach post haste. It was no wonder he didn't remember seeing Kendall around.

"And you went to Heartfalls University?"

"I did. With Emma and Daisy."

"Did you guys have the same major?"

"No way. I majored in English Lit. Emma in education with an English emphasis. And Daisy earned a couple of humanity majors. She enjoyed taking the classes to annoy her parents."

He laughed. "I can imagine that."

"Gotta love her."

"I just recently started hanging out with her husband. Seems like a cool guy."

"Yeah. He's kind of quiet, but you can see the love he has for Daisy in his eyes."

Did Q's eyes say that about Kendall? Would she even notice if they did?

"Seems like your major is treating you well."

She beamed. "I love it. Now if only I can own a home one day large enough to house all of my books." She motioned around the flat. "As you can imagine, I can't store a lot of books in here."

"I see you have a few stacks going on." He pointed to the ones he had noticed. The ones on each end table flanking the couch. The stack by the entrance table. And the one in the corner on the floor.

"Yeah but I have nowhere to put them once I'm done reading. I already put a bookshelf in the closet."

He almost spit soup all over himself. Q grabbed a napkin to wipe his face. "You took up closet space to hold a bookshelf?"

"If I had the stamina, I'd put shelving on the walls to hold all my books."

"Seriously?"

She leaned forward, a solemn expression on her face. "Quite."

"Then I'll do it for you."

~

Kendall gaped at the man sitting across from her. First, he'd shoveled her porch. Now he was offering to hang shelves for her books. Her heart flopped in her chest and a weird feeling spread throughout it. It couldn't be love. She didn't know him well enough to commit. But if she wasn't ready for that type of relationship, now would be the time to abort before he held her heart in his hands.

She took a sip of water in attempt to still her nerves. "That would be nice, but I don't want to take time away from Deuce."

"I make time for people who are important to me." His brown eyes bore into hers.

Any moment now, she'd swoon from the romance of it all. How could she keep her cool when Q went around saying things like that or writing notes that melted her heart?

But was it true?

Her emotions must have displayed across her face because Q reached across the table and held her hand. "I don't say anything I don't mean. You're important to me, and if shelving will make you happy and your home less cluttered," he winked. "Then I'll grab some shelves from the hobby store."

"I can buy them."

"So can I." He let her hand go and bit the last of his bread.

"You're already providing the labor, so I'll provide the supplies."

"How about I buy everything since I offered?"

"Halfsies?"

His lips twitched, and then a full smile broke out. "You're stubborn."

"And you like me."

"That I do."

Kendall finished the rest of her soup as Q took his dishes to the sink and began washing them. She wanted to squeal and give a mental pinch of her arm. How could a man be this good?

Maybe Ty was just that bad.

She suppressed a sigh. It was a depressing thought to think she chose so horribly the first time around, but it was also a little bit of a boon. Maybe that meant she'd grown. She'd finally let Christ do the work in her life, completing her instead of expecting a man to. It allowed her to appreciate the good qualities in Q instead of expecting them constantly.

But she was still a little afraid of letting go completely. It was no mistake; she *had* chosen badly for her first marriage. One she thought was going to be 'til death did them part, but one she frankly was relieved it wasn't. This time, caution would either help the situation or hurt it.

She could only pray that Quinton hadn't lied when he said he'd wait.

He turned and leaned back against the sink. "I'm going to check on the porch and snow fall."

"All right."

"I'm going to stay down there once I'm finished."

She blinked, trying to hide the hurt. "Oh?"

"It's nothing you did." He walked forward. "I just need to be able to keep my mind from entertaining temptation."

Her mouth dropped open as her cheeks heated. "Oh," she drew out. She tempted him like that? "I can bring you dinner when it's ready. We can eat down there if that helps."

He ran a hand across his chin. "That's probably best. Hopefully they'll be able to dig us out tomorrow."

"Will Deuce be okay without you?" She hated that he

couldn't go home to his son. Even if part of her was pleased she got to spend more time with him.

"Yeah. I'm sure Gran is keeping him occupied. If anything, it's my dad and Gran who need me, not Deuce. He has enough energy to keep us all on our toes."

Kendall leaned against her chair. If this thing between her and Q kept up, would she one day be Deuce's step-mom? She blinked rapidly. Should she ask him what he was expecting? He did declare love.

"Are you going to tell me what's got the smoke coming out of your ears?" His mouth quirked to the side as if he were hiding a bigger grin.

"It's about Deuce."

His open gaze watched her patiently.

"And me. Well, us. I mean..."

He held a hand up. "I'm in this for keeps, but I'm not going to do anything that is too much or too fast for either one of you."

Duh, Kendall. It's not just about you. Quinton had to ensure that she wasn't a flight risk like his—

Her eyes flew to his. "Are you worried I'll leave?"

"No." Q sat back down. "I was in the beginning, but God helped remind me that I can't live in fear. You're not my ex-wife just like I'm not your ex-husband. I can't enter a relationship with you and punish you or rather, react in a way that blames you for my ex's crimes."

Her shoulders relaxed.

"But at the same time, I can't introduce you to Deuce as his stepmom and expect you to discipline him or care for him as if we've been a family forever."

He wanted to be a family. Her heart flopped right along with her stomach. "I understand."

"You do?"

She nodded. "I'm not your ex but I'm not your wife either. I get it, Q."

He winced. "That sounds harsh."

"I didn't mean it to be. I'm just trying to say you'll handle whatever relationship Deuce and I will have in those parameters."

"I will. And I promise to share my thoughts with you. I don't want you to freak out," he paused, his eyes shining with acceptance. "But I do want forever with you. That includes rings, vows, and happily ever after. And God willing, you and Deuce will have a relationship I could only dream of."

Tears smarted her eyes. Q was so considerate. She leaned across the table, steadying herself with her hands pressed against the top. Quinton's eyes widened when he realized her intentions. Closing hers, Kendall kissed him with all the affection her heart wished to pour out.

Chapter Seventeen

"Family not only need to consist of merely those whom we share blood, but also for those whom we'd give blood."
— Charles Dickens

"Merry Christmas!" Deuce shouted with delight as he pounced on Quinton's stomach.

Q gasped for air. "My stomach, Deuce!"

"Sorry, Daddy." Deuce wiggled off of him and laid next to Q's side. "Are you going to lay here all morning?"

"No." Q shook his head. "I was just thinking." He would be meeting Kendall's mom for the first time and couldn't shake the worry of making a good impression.

"Thinking about your presents?"

"No," he chuckled. He stared down at his son, loving the innocence and joy that shone on his face.

"Thinking about Christmas dinner?"

"Kind of." Because Kendall and her mom would be joining them.

"I like the presents more than the food."

No kidding. "You mean you don't want to eat any candied yams?"

Deuce looked up at him. "Is that the orange stuff with the marshmallows?"

"It is."

"Okay. I like the food too." Deuce patted his belly then peered up at him. "But you can't play with it, just the toys."

"How do you know you're getting toys?"

Deuce rolled his eyes. "You always get me toys." He frowned. "Right?"

"Sometimes I get you books."

"Don't do that this year." Deuce shuddered. "Ms. Kendall probably bought me some."

Q smiled against his son's head. "She might have." He loved how much the two got along.

"Do you think she'll like our present?" Deuce squeezed Q's arm in a hug.

"I think so."

"Good, because we can't keep a bookshelf. No room." Deuce sat up, kneeling on the mattress. "I think we should go open presents."

"Gran and Grandpa are probably still sleeping."

"Nuh uh. Gran is cooking."

Q sniffed the air. *Huh.* He could smell some type of bread baking. Guess she was up. "And Grandpa?"

"Reading the newspaper in his chair."

"Then I'll get up."

"And we'll open presents?" Deuce clasped his hands in a begging motion.

"Yes."

"Finally!" Deuce ran out of Q's room.

Q blinked as this morning's conversation with Deuce rolled through his memory bank. He adjusted his tie one last time before pulling his sweater vest over his shirt and tie. Usually he dressed more casually for Christmas, but that was before he'd invited Kendall and her mom. He needed to make a good impression. What would her mom be like? Kind? Mean? Somewhere in between? Q sighed, rubbing his brow. What he really wanted to know was how her absence affected Kendall.

Time will tell.

He missed seeing Kendall sitting across the table from him. Once the snow had stopped and had been shoveled, Q had returned home and back to his normal everyday routine. The days had flown by and now Christmas greeted them.

Later that afternoon, Q walked into his room to make sure he was presentable for Kendall's impending visit. He smiled as he remembered Deuce's face while opening his presents. His son had loved every toy under the tree. His Gran and Dad had enjoyed their gifts as well. Dad had given Q a year's subscription to his favorite magazine. Gran had bought him some hats and sweaters. She always felt that men should dress like gentleman, especially when they were courting.

Her words not his.

Too bad he couldn't wear one of his new hats to dinner. It would shield his eyes and match his sweater vest.

"Boy, stop preening in front of that mirror," Gran said,

an arthritic hand on her hip. "Kendall's car just pulled into the driveway."

"Thanks, Gran." He paused, kissing her on the cheek then rushed to the front of the house.

He arrived at the front door just as the doorbell peeled.

Lord, please let this go well. I pray that Kendall's mom likes me and my family. I pray that we're all relaxed around one another. Amen.

Q opened the door and smiled brightly. "Merry Christmas, ladies."

"Merry Christmas."

"Come on in." He moved to the side so they could enter, and then shut the door.

Kendall gestured to her right. "Q, this is my mom, Karol Jackson. Mom, this is Quinton Hendricks."

"Nice to meet you, Ms. Jackson." He shook her hand, hoping his palms weren't a disgusting clammy mess. He couldn't remember ever being this nervous when meeting a girlfriend's parent before.

"Same here, Quinton."

"Daddy!"

Q turned in time to brace for impact as Deuce barreled into his legs. He ducked his head when he noticed Kendall's mom. "Deuce, meet Kendall's mom."

He peeked out. "Merry Christmas," he mumbled.

"Merry Christmas and nice to meet you." Kendall's mom squatted to Deuce's level. "I remember when Kendall was your height."

His eyes widened. "But she's big."

Kendall met Q's eyes, her face soft with happiness.

"She hasn't always been that tall. She used to walk

around with a thumb in her mouth and a book in the other hand."

Deuce giggled. "She still likes books."

"Have you been to The Cozy Shelf?"

He nodded.

"Want to tell me about it?"

"Okay." He let go of Q's legs and held on to Kendall's mother's hand. They walked toward the living room, forgetting Q and Kendall existed.

"I've never seen him do something like that."

"My mom has a way with kids. All the practice working on flights."

He slid his hands around her waist. "Merry Christmas, beautiful."

"Merry Christmas." She slid her hands around his neck and met his lips.

He took his time greeting her. It had been too long since their last kiss. Two days to be exact.

Kendall broke away, her breaths coming in short waves. "Hello to you too." She winked at him.

"I might have missed you a little bit."

"You'd think being snowed in with me would have sent you running for the hills." She started to walk toward the living room.

"I'm not going anywhere."

She paused, turning her head to peer into his eyes. "I know." And then she walked away.

Q leaned against the door, letting out an exhale. The trust that had shined in her eyes almost undid him. She finally believed him. Finally trusted he would wait.

Merry Christmas to me.

Kendall laughed at Deuce's knock-knock joke. It had ended with him singing about Santa Claus coming to town. She looked around the table and thanked God.

Last year, Christmas had seemed so isolating. She had spent it with Daisy and Emma, but she had been very conscious that she was alone. Her mother had been stuck in Hawaii, enjoying an extra-long layover. But now, her mother sat at the same table as Q and his family.

As if they were all part of the same family.

"Now to Him who is able to do exceedingly abundantly above all that we ask or think..."

God had answered her desire to have something more. She had thought that owning The Cozy Shelf was all she needed in life, but He knew better. He could see the deepest desire of her heart. And how could He not? As much as Kendall read romance books, it had become apparent that she desired to be romanced and loved for who God created her to be.

He'd answered that in the gift of Q. In the blessing of Deuce's acceptance as a permanent fixture in his dad's life. He'd even brought her mother home for Christmas.

And every moment had been treasured.

She and her mom had eaten cereal for Christmas Eve dinner as they'd watched Christmas movie after Christmas movie. For the first time in a long time, Kendall had stopped viewing her mom in the lens of her past and chose to enjoy her presence in the now.

It made all the difference. They had sat around and just talked. Her mother had listened to her gush about Q and Deuce. She'd even bought them a Christmas present. Granted it had come from The Cozy Shelf since it had been a last minute thought, but still, her mother had the thought.

What had surprised Kendall most of all was her Christmas present. For once, it wasn't some elaborate piece of jewelry, but one that could have been made by a toddler. Her mother had turned the marshmallows from their favorite cereal into a bracelet charm. Kendall had cried from laughing so hard.

God had been blessing her left and right.

They finished their meal and then made their way into the living room. Mr. Hendricks sat in a leather recliner, reaching for the Bible that laid on the end table. "Kendall, Karol, it's our tradition to read the second chapter of Luke in celebration of Christ's birth."

"And then we eat cake," Deuce announced, excitement ramping his voice up an octave.

Deuce snuggled in Q's lap and leaned his head back against his dad. Q held out his hand in the space between them. She intertwined her fingers with his, resting her head on his shoulder.

Deuce turned and looked down at their hands, and then up at her. "I don't get to hold your hand too?"

Her lip quivered as she tempered her emotions. "Of course you can."

"Good." He smiled and laid his hand on top of theirs as Q's father started reading.

Merry Christmas to me.

Epilogue

"Forever is composed of nows." — Emily Dickinson

Valentine's Day

Kendall stood in front of her closet. *What to wear, what to wear?* Q would be taking her out to celebrate Valentine's Day. They had rung in the New Year together and enjoyed each other's company in all the days between. Funny how a simple change in year could have her reflecting on a new life, have new hopes, new dreams.

And all of them involved a handsome mechanic and his adorable son.

She reached for the red long-sleeved dress. It would go great with black tights and her cream ankle booties. After donning her outfit, she checked her reflection in the mirror. The red scarf she'd wrapped around her hair, leaving tufts of it hanging out at the top looked fantastic. She felt date-ready.

A few minutes later, Kendall walked down the stairs to meet Q. She smiled when she saw him leaning against the porch railing. Apparently he had been there for a while.

I wonder why he didn't just text me?

She opened the door, quickly locking it behind her.

"Hey, there." He kissed her on the forehead. "Happy Valentine's Day."

"Happy Valentine's Day to you too."

He smiled and wrapped her hand in his. "Come on. Dinner awaits." He led her down the steps and to the side of his truck. She paused, mouth dropping open.

"You painted it."

"Sure did. You like?"

"I love." The matte black finish added so much character.

Q opened the door for her, leaning against it.

Kendall stepped down the sidewalk onto the street and stopped. On the seat was a stack of books that had been wrapped in ribbon, a bow on the very top. "What's this?"

"Your present."

She picked up the stack, turning them to read the spines. "Q," she whispered.

He'd gifted her *The Hobbit* and *Lord of the Rings* collection.

"Thank you so much." She turned to him, wrapping him in a one-arm hug.

"My pleasure, Kendall." He ran a finger down her cheek and kissed her softly on the lips.

Kendall pulled back and looked into his eyes. *Forever is composed of nows.* The quote from Emily Dickinson drifted in her mind. Every single day, Quinton showed up. Whether it was to take her out on a date, to take his son to story time and then sharing a muffin or two with her afterward, or simply sending her a text that let her know he was thinking of her.

Not a day had gone by since his declaration without him showing in some way that he loved her. And now it was her turn.

"I love you, Quinton Hendricks."

The cheek-splitting, dimple-flashing grin brightened his face. He cupped her cheek and kissed her deeply. "I love you, too," he rasped.

He pulled back and reached into his jacket pocket, pulling out a card. The same kind he had used to leave notes to her. "I have one final card to give you." He took her books and gave her the card.

Anticipation had her foot tapping a rhythm on the pavement as her hands shook trying to open the envelope. Finally, she lifted the card out and opened it.

"Forever is composed of nows."

Pure joy lit her heart. If she had any doubts that loving Q was worth it, this confirmed every hope of her heart.

"It's perfect."

"I love you now and forever."

"Now and forever," she whispered.

A letter to the reader

Dear Reader Friend,

Thank you so much for taking a journey with me to Heartfalls, New York. I had fun dreaming up this fictional town and those who lived there. In fact, I had so much fun I'm planning on returning there to revisit some friends you met in *Deck the Shelves.*

But until that time, I pray that you felt God's presence in Kendall and Quinton's story. I pray you enjoyed all that endears us to Christmas and of course, all things bookish.

I would love it if you would leave a review for the novella collection and spread the word. If you wish to read any of my other stories, please check out my book list and sign up to receive my newsletters.

Blessings,

Toni Shiloh

Acknowledgments

To my husband and boys: thank you for blessing me with time to write! I love you all.

To Dawn Marie Pitts: thanks for giving me Deuce's nickname!

To Kelly Goshorn: thank you for helping me name the rooms in The Cozy Shelf! I appreciate you!

To my critique partners: thank you Andrea Boyd and Sarah Monzon for helping me make this story better than the rough draft I sent you. Love you guys!

To my readers: you make this journey so worth it. Thanks for encouraging me, reviewing the books, and blessing me with your time on social media!

About the Author

Toni Shiloh is a wife, mom, and Christian contemporary romance author. Once she understood the powerful saving grace thanks to the love of Christ, she was moved to honor her Savior. She writes to bring Him glory and to learn more about His goodness.

She spends her days hanging out with her husband and their two boys. She is a member of the American Christian Fiction Writers (ACFW) and president of the Virginia Chapter.

You can find her on her website at http://tonishiloh.-wordpress.com. Signup for her Book News newsletter at http://eepurl.com/gcMfqT.

More Books by Toni Shiloh

Short Novels

The Maple Run Series

Buying Love

Finding Love

Enduring Love

Novels

The Freedom Lake Series

Returning Home

Grace Restored

Finally Accepted

Novellas

A Life to Live

A Spring of Weddings

A Sidelined Christmas